SC RISING

A Seaside Noir

And there is an aspect of the sign of
SCORPIO, spur'd & driven by Evil,
that answers Viciousness with Viciousness
& which the passage of TIME but does
seldom commute.

– THE ROYAL & AUTHENTICK MERLIN (1835)

NO EXIT PRESS

First published in Great Britain by No Exit Press, 1999,
18 Coleswood Road, Harpenden, Herts, AL5 1EQ.

http://www.noexit.co.uk

A CIP catalogue record for this book is available from the British Library.

ISBN 1 901982-53-X Scorpian Rising

2   4   6   8   10   9   7   5   3   1

Typography by the author.
Typeset in Palatino by Koinonia, Manchester
and printed and bound in Great Britain by
Caledonian International Book Manufacturing, Glasgow.

For Eileen Gallagher
and Mike Hodges

1: Jumpin' with Symphony Sid

THE LARGE MERCEDES saloon with smoked glass windows pulled out of the racecourse and headed back to London. It was a good Thursday because Sidney Blattner who was sitting in the back, flanked by his two aides, Vince and young Leo, had cleaned up on the horses and was now some £60,000 better off than when he awoke this morning in the arms of Barbara, one of his mistresses, down in St George's Square, behind Victoria Station. A good Thursday all right, but it wouldn't be for long. Today things would, in a phrase much favoured by Sid but usually applied to others, start to come unstuck.

Not just unstuck.

But, to use the medial emphatic also favoured by Sid, un-*fucking*-stuck.

Sid Blattner was sixty-two years of age and a very successful London criminal. For some years now he had been
going into legitimate ventures with the cash that had
cascaded in from protection rackets, drugs, girls, gambling
and all the rest of the bent ventures gallimaufry. He knew
where he was going and he thought he knew how he was
going to get there. He was always like that – organised,
methodical, wily. And he considered himself untouchable
because he had linked himself with so many figures in
public life that to bring him down you would have to
bring *them* down too.

The whole house of cards in other words.

And nobody was going to risk *that*.

Good insurance.

Luck, however, had played a larger part in Sid's life
than most people realised, least of all Sid himself who, like
most successful men, refused to acknowledge its existence
in any way as a contributing factor.

Today, that luck was running out and Sid's life was to
begin unravelling, but as the Merc crossed Chelsea Bridge
he was as unaware of this turn in his fortune as he was of
the fate of the horse that won him the £60,000 – it died of a
heart attack immediately after the race, having been
injected with a little too much of the old go-fast syrup.

Yeah, £60,000 better off. Not bad, not bad at all, Sid thought
to himself. Well pleased.

'Nothing like a good gamble!' says Sid, voicing his inner
thoughts.

'Hardly a gamble…when you know what the result's
gonna be,' noted Vince.

'That don't reduce the *sporting* element. Anything could
go wrong. It's still a gamble no matter what anyone says,'
Sid replied.

'Yeah, it's still a gamble,' echoed Leo and then, as an
afterthought, in deep philosophical mode, 'but then life's a
gamble itself, ain't it?'

'You, Leo, my old son, have never spoken a truer word,' replied Sid.

Leo smiled and said, 'You've got to say it as it is.'

Vince gazed out at the Thames and thought to himself, these two sound like characters out of a daytime TV soap opera, they really do. Then Vince's eye returned to the Thames and he thought that the flowing waters here could take him down to the estuary and the sea and the sea could take him up the east coast to Wells...Wells-next-the-Sea, to give it its full name. The water *here* is connected with the water *there*. Just one boat trip and he'd be there. One day he would do it, quit London for good, and sooner rather than later, he hoped.

He had promised himself he would do it before his fortieth birthday. And that only left him eighteen months. Not long at all.

Sid knocked back the glass of champagne and fanned some of the cash. He loved the feel of it. Truly he did. There was something about the physical texture of it that made him excited – generally excited to begin with, then sexually excited. It got him going and it did right now. He'd pop over and see Barbara again, give her one. Yeah. Give her a right seeing to. Right now.

Yeah, he could do with a bit of her.

Her eyes burned like 1000-watt bulbs whenever he turned up with a fistful of Jack Dash. She's a turbo-driven slut when there's cash about. I'll have some of her, thought Sid, right *now*.

Sid told Harry the Chauffeur to make for St George's Square.

Leo asked, 'You going to see your Barbara?'

'Yeah,' nodded Sid. 'I can drop you two off at the underground or you can sit it out in the car...suit yourselves on this one.'

'We're not going there, guv,' said Vince softly.

'Why's that, then, son?' demanded Sid.

Vince replied, 'Because there's a problem.'

'A problem? You know I try and run this organisation without problems? You know that.'

'Right, guv. But we got one this time. And he's called Brian Spinks.'

'Oh, yeah…that toe-rag!'

'Yeah.'

'Vince, it should be like a symphony, shouldn't it?'

'A symphony, Sid. Yes.'

'We all do our little bit as instructed in harmony *and* on time and we make *music*. But when we don't, there's discord and *no* music.'

'Couldn't express it better myself,' said Vince as he yawned and thought to himself, how many times have I heard that little bit of phraseology from Sid? I'd be a rich man if I had a couple of pennies for every time I've heard that fly out of his mouth.

After a pause Sid banged his fist into the open palm of his other hand and hissed, 'I knew that Brian Spinks was a wrong 'un.'

I told you so, thought Vince to himself. I *told* you so, but you never bothered to listen.

And a symphony, indeed!

Vince had been working for Sid for some fifteen years now, ever since he came out of the army. Too long to stay in one job, particularly one like this, thought Vince. He was getting stale and he knew it. The glamour had worn pretty thin. Working for Sid had cost him his marriage and he didn't want it to cost him anything else.

He'd accepted Sid's original offer and had intended only staying a few months until he got on his feet. But he was still here all these years later and going nowhere fast or, as his girlfriend put it, going nowhere *slow*.

The job back then had been a big step up for a working-class kid from Drury Lane, but where had it got him?

Brian Spinks' common law wife was pushed in the stomach as she opened the door of the basement flat in Kentish

Town, then she was punched in the face as the lad himself, Brian, was bundled out and up the steps and into the back of a grimy van that sped off up Leighton Road.

By the time the van reached York Way Brian was trussed up, thin hemp rope cutting into his wrists and ankles. And the blindfold wasn't contributing to his well-being either.

This was not the way Brian had envisaged spending the rest of his thirtieth birthday. No, he and June were going out to get a couple of videos and some Chinese take-away and have a quiet evening in. He didn't expect this.

'What's it all about?' cried Brian who had recognised his abductors. 'What've I done then?'

Phil the Enforcer stubbed out his cigarette on Brian's neck and said, 'You've upset Symphony Sid, you have. That's enough…ain't it?'

Brian's screams were buried beneath the siren of a passing police car sent to investigate an attempted hold-up in an Indian corner shop somewhere on the Caledonian Road.

The Merc headed east along the Embankment.

'There's always some little toe-rag like Spinks who just ain't satisfied. There always is, isn't there?' declared Sid.

Leo murmured agreement.

'Shit for brains,' added Vince, still thinking of Wells and the sea.

The van drove through the gates of the scrap-metal yard that somewhat grandiosely declared itself to passers-by in Dalston Junction as being ALBION NON-FERROUS METALS [1947] LTD. Once inside the vehicle pulled up by the docking bay and Phil and his two helpers, Kenny the Driver and Slim, picked up Spinks, manhandled him on to a sack-barrow and wheeled him over to the lift and up to the first floor.

'I ain't done nothing,' shouted Brian prior to Kenny the Driver kicking him in the ribs.

'You're a transgressor, mate,' said Phil. 'Know that? A fuckin' *transgressor*.'

The Merc pulled into the scrap-yard and Vince got out first, looked around and then signalled to Sid and Leo that it was OK for them to get out too. They then hurried across to the docking bay and into the lift.

Sid opened the door of what used to be the chairman's office and nodded to the three droogs who silently greeted him.

'Well done, lads,' said Sid as he went over to Spinks who was now naked and spread-eagled with his face against the wall, his arms and wrists tied severely to Harlan No. 3 wall-anchors.

Spinks looks over his shoulder and says, 'Hello, Mr B. They've got it wrong, they have.'

'We've got nothing wrong,' spits Sid. 'You've not only been doing a bit of freelance work without a licence from me, you've also been skimming the two clubs!'

'What me? Not *me*, Mr B!'

'Yes, *you*. And Vince here reckons we're down about ten grand because of your unprincipled greed…so you're going to have to be chastised. Understand? Phil here is going to dish out a bit of medicine.'

Phil cracks a bull-whip in the air. The crack echoes throughout the room and down the passage that now echoes also with the footfalls of Harry the Chauffeur as he runs to the end office, his face red and flustered.

'What is it?' says Sid, turning to Harry and irritated by the interruption.

Harry gets his breath back and says, 'Telephone in the car, boss. Very important. It's the wife.'

Sid looks at Harry and then at Vince and then Sid walks out the room with Vince following him as the first of many lashes bites into Spinks' back.

Miriam Blattner was sitting on the leather sofa with a tele-

phone in one hand and a Marlboro cigarette in the other,
her bright red, false fingernails glistening in the light from
the angled wall-mounting behind her. Her feet were on the
reproduction Louis Quinze-style coffee table and her mind
was on the projected Miami holiday she was going to take
later in the week with her sister (married to a ne'er-do-well
on the fringes of the schmatte industry, a shlemiel according to Sid who would have a bath and forget to wash his
face).

'Sid? No, I'm fine…I just got a call from the police…I
don't know…the Kent police, down in Margate…yes…it's
Lionel…he's dead…I got the name and number here. Call
him…some police constable. Found dead this morning…I
was in the middle of something…couldn't get all the
details. *You* phone them.'

Sid lit a cheroot and paced up and down the yard as Vince
sat in the car and called the police down in Margate.

Sid couldn't understand it. How could Lionel be dead?
A bit overweight perhaps but always in good health.
Never a day's illness in his life. Strong as an ox. Stronger.
Perhaps it wasn't his health? Perhaps he was in a car
crash? Fell off a ladder. Got food poisoning or something?
But dead? Not Lionel. No, never. He couldn't be…*dead*.
Not his brother.

Vince returned the car-phone to its cradle, got out the
car and looked around. Sid was over the far side of the
yard leaning against a wheel-less 2.8 litre Ford Granada
puffing on the cheroot like it was the last one he'd ever
have.

Sid ain't prepared for this, thought Vince. He's prepared
for just about everything, but he ain't prepared for this.
None of us are.

Sid looked up at the approaching Vince. 'What's the
strength of it then?'

Vince was silent. He stared at Sid and then lit up a
cigarette and gazed across the yard.

'Come on, I ain't got all day. What happened down there?' Sid demanded.

Down there, thought Vince, who knows what went on? But something did. Old Lionel, as straight as Sid is bent. Not an enemy in the world. Never left home, helped their mum run the corner newsagent's, nursed her through her terminal illness, carried on running the shop, never married. Poor old Lionel. The most exciting thing he ever did was fill out the coupons for the football pools. Who'd have ever thought Sid and him were brothers?

But this was serious, deadly serious. Either that or a chronic case of mistaken identity.

No, there was a smell to this. An uncomfortable odour.

Sid screamed, 'Are you going to tell me or am I gonna have to phone those fucking swedes myself?!'

'This is going to be a big shock for you, Sid. A big one.'

'It is, is it?'

'It is.'

'What then?'

'Lionel was found on the beach….'

'Yeah?'

'On the beach – bound up.'

'Bound up?'

'And not only that – executed.'

'*Executed*?'

'Yeah. A bullet through his forehead at point blank range.'

Sid slumped against the car. 'This can't be true! He never did anyone any harm…ever!'

'I think we better be going now,' said Vince as he put his arm around Sid and led him back to the car in silence.

Harry the Chauffeur turned off Totteridge Lane and through the automatic gates (with heraldic lions on each pillar high above the security fencing) and pulled to a near-silent halt at the front of Sidiam, Sid's twelve-bedroom architect-designed *Dallas*-style house, the name of which came from a partial conjunction of his and his wife's names (behind

Sid's back the lads always referred to the house as Miridney).

Vince helped Sid out the car. Miriam wasn't at home to offer her comfort as she'd gone to some designer dress evening in Hendon, but the barely English-speaking Filipino couple were there with the roast beef, Sid's favourite dish when he wasn't in mourning, when he wasn't grieving, when he wasn't in a right two-and-eight.

Sid grabbed a half-bottle of brandy and knocked it back in half-a-dozen swigs and then he fell on the bed and passed out.

Vince checked out the house and the grounds and then went to the spare bedroom at the top of the stairs. If anything were to happen tonight he'd be the first to know.

But nothing did.

Lionel's execution was enough.

The next morning, at around eleven o'clock, Sid slouched into the breakfast room in his silk dressing gown and Moroccan slippers. Vince looked up from the *Sun* and his big fry-up and said, 'How you feeling, guv?'

Sid sat down opposite him and lit a cigarette and said, 'All shook up, I am.'

'Yeah, understandable.'

'Mrs B, sir, gone to work-out club,' said Maria the Filipino housekeeper.

'Yeah,' said Sid in reply, 'and you got a strawberry milk-shake, Maria?'

'*Si*, sir,' she replied.

'There's a bit here in the *Sun*,' says Vince, pushing the tabloid across the large circular table.

Sid glances at it and says, 'I can't concentrate. What's it say?'

'No more than we know already. Says Lionel was well respected and that.'

'Any mention of me?'

'Yeah, they just say you're his brother, that you're a prominent London businessman.'

'That all?'

'Yeah. Nothing else.'

'Who we got in Fleet Street who'd know what the Old Bill down there is up to?'

'Wallace Slade's the guy for this,' murmurs Vince as he wipes the plate with a slice of white bread.

'Yeah, good old Wally. He owes us, don't he?'

'Sure does.'

'I want him at the club this evening. And I want him with information.'

'*Information*. Got you, guv. And there's somebody else I can try too.'

'Good.'

Vince pushed open the door of the Grape Tree wine bar and through the smoke saw good old Wally at the bar regaling a couple of young reporters with, no doubt, half-invented stories about his great days of crime reporting chasing after the Messinas or the Krays or the Richardsons or whoever. That's all he ever rabbited on about.

'Hello, Wally,' says Vince.

'Vincent, dear boy. What a pleasant surprise to see you here. You must try this Haut-Brion. You simply must!'

Vince whispers in his ear, 'No time right now, Wally. I want a word with you outside.'

'Outside?'

'Right. And now, if you please.'

'Gentlemen, you must excuse me for a moment. Duty calls!'

Vince hated Wally's upper-class accent almost as much as he hated Wally's bow-ties and decorative waistcoats. In fact he hated Wally – *period*. How this wanker could ever end up being a chief crime correspondent was beyond Vince's ken. Indeed, it was beyond most people's ken.

Once outside Wally says, 'A bit of a rude interruption, old man. Know what I mean? Just not on coming in like that. Not *on* at all.'

Vince ignored Wally's remark and asked him if he had heard about Sid's brother. He had. Did he know anything more? No, he didn't.

'Well, in that case, Wal, you're gonna find out more, aren't you? And Sid wants you around the club at six. OK?'

'Steady on, old man. I'm at a crime correspondents' dinner tonight.'

'Not any more you're not. *You* are at the club.'

'This happened down in Kent, in Margate. It's not the Met down there. I've got no contacts.'

'You better start developing them then, eh?'

'I can't just pick up the phone and — '

'*Do* what you have to *do*. Sid wants *information* and he wants it tonight. You understand?'

'I hardly think....'

Wally's voice trailed off as Vince stepped out on to the road and hailed a cab.

The cab pulled up opposite the main entrance to New Scotland Yard. Vince looked out the window and across. A tall, distinguished figure in a white raincoat emerged from the main entrance, glanced in Vince's direction, and hurriedly walked across the road to the cab. Vince opened the door for him. This was Chief-Superintendent Lucksford.

The Chief-Super said, 'This is a bit out of order. Calling me up like this.'

'Needs must...when the devil drives,' says Vince in reply and then, leaning forward to the cabby, 'Take us round the block.'

The cabby waves an assent as Vince slides the window behind him shut.

'I take it this is about Sid's brother?' says Lucksford.

'Hole in one. What you heard?'

'Only what I've read in the papers. Nothing more.'

'Sid wants the full story. He wants to know what's going on. He wants all the *detail*, and now.'

'They're Kent, not the Met. They're a different breed of men *down there*.'

Down there. Everybody talks about Margate being *down there*. Christ, Vince thought to himself, Margate's only sixty-odd miles out of London on the coast. They all talk about it like it's another country.

'What can I tell you, Chief-Super? Harry wants the inside track and he wants it tonight. Try not to disappoint him.'

Lucksford sighed.

Vince smiled at him and said, 'Sid's been a good mate to you, Brian. Hasn't he? He don't often ask you for a favour, eh?'

'I'll try not to let him down,' replied the Chief-Super.

After the Chief-Super was dropped off at a discreet distance from his offices the cabby headed to Sid's casino off Curzon Street. Vince was sitting in the back of the cab a worried man. Lionel's murder – correction, Lionel's *execution* – was a bit too much. This really couldn't be a case of mistaken identity, not down there. Not down there...in Margate of all places. That half-asleep, dead-and-alive, cheap seaside resort. No. Punch-ups between drunks at closing time and the odd slashing between spotty youths fighting over the favours of some blonde-from-a-bottle Sharon were the limit of it. Nobody was trussed up and shot in the head down there. Nobody. Ever.

But Lionel was.

He certainly fucking was.

Could Lionel have been involved in something we didn't know about? No. No way. Vince had known Lionel as long as he had known Sid, over twenty years. There were no dark secrets in Lionel's life. The guy was as you saw him.

Wasn't he?

Lionel ran the newsagent's after his mother died, and what else? Not much else at all. Kept to himself and went bowling sometimes with the geriatric set. The highlight of his week was probably reading the obits in the *Jewish Chronicle*. That was it. A quiet, introspective guy. End of story.

Vince had an uncomfortable feeling that this was merely the start of —

No, it couldn't be....

He hoped he was wrong.

Of course he was.

Crazy even thinking that.

The accountants and lawyers gathered up their papers and shuffled out of the boardroom some three floors above Sid's Velvet Casino and Sporting Club.

Sid lit a cheroot and walked over to the window. He pressed his face against the glass of a pane on the far right and squinted down past Curzon Street. 'If you stand here like this you can just make out Hyde Park.'

'Fancy that,' replies Vince.

'Yeah.'

Sid returned to the boardroom table and poured himself another coffee from the silver pot. 'You want some, Vince?'

'I got some. Thanks.'

'I'll tell you – whatever else they might say about this operation any place I run does *bloody* good coffee. None of that *catering* shit.'

'The best,' observes Vince, 'and how did the meeting go?'

'Pretty good. The Bournemouth casino is on time and the take-over of the amusement park in Great Yarmouth seems certain. But I told them, the massed ranks of the Royal Institute of Grey Suits, that we've got to set up some new laundering schemes. The money from the skims and the odd licensed operation and so on is mounting up faster than we can deal with it. It's getting embarrassing.'

Vince could tell by the nineteen-to-the-dozen way Sid was talking that he was doing everything to stop himself thinking about Lionel. This was Sid's way whenever some tragedy struck – keep busy, immerse yourself in work, don't stop talking. It was the same when his mother died. The same when Miriam was involved in the car crash and the surgeons didn't know whether she would live or die. The same when Lionel went in for that operation last year....

Yeah, it was the same.

But facts have to be faced.

'Wally boy's downstairs,' volunteered Vince.

'Let's have him up then,' Sid said brusquely.

Vince reached over to the phone and dialled a couple of numbers and said OK to whoever answered it.

'Leo'll be up with him in a jiff.'

Sid puffed on his cheroot and said, 'We're going to get to the bottom of this and we're going to do it fast. You understand?'

'We'll get it sorted,' said Vince, but there was little confidence in his voice.

Sid walked over to the window and again peered up and down the street while Vince finished his coffee. There was an eerie quietness up here above the street. Right bang in the centre of London, but not a sound. It was an eerier silence, Vince thought, because things are not as they should be. Something was badly wrong, and he couldn't put his finger on it.

The doors opened and Wally marches in puffing on a cigar. Vince could smell the liquor on him at this distance. Leo indicated to Wally to sit down at the head of the table and then closed the double doors.

'My deepest sympathies to you at this time,' gushes Wally as he takes a seat. Sid turns from the window and nods at Wally and then looks at Vince. Vince takes his cue and says, 'Right, Wally, old boy. What you got?'

'Not an awful lot, old man. Frightfully difficult getting information from *that* quarter, you know.'

Sid has turned his back on the room. He's looking out the window again, probably keeping an eye on Hyde Park, but he's still listening.

Vince taps his fingers on the table and says quietly, patiently, 'We're all listening.'

'Your late brother was found on the beach at Margate yesterday morning, about 7 a.m., by two unemployed seasonal workers who were going beach-combing or something. They alerted the police.'

'And?' says Sid. Not allowing Wally to take a breath.

'And...uh...they phoned the police right away. The police were there within minutes and they made an ID. Your brother had his wallet on him with a driving licence and some cash-and-carry card with a photograph. The ID was also confirmed by a couple of constables who knew him and a Mrs Spooner who worked for him in the shop. He'd been shot in the forehead at virtually point blank range with a .45 pistol. He had about £300 in fifties and twenties on him. They hadn't taken that.'

Sid turned to Vince and said, 'It wasn't a robbery then.'

Vince nodded his head in agreement and thought, did we ever think it was?

Sid's getting impatient: 'What else?'

Wally drains the last drops of brandy from his hip flask and wipes his mouth on the sleeve of his jacket. 'Mrs Spooner was the last person to see him alive, it appears. She left the shop at about 6.30 p.m. on Wednesday evening. He locked up and, presumably, went upstairs to the flat. Nobody saw anything – at the shop, at the beach, anywhere. Least nobody's come forward yet.'

Vince wanted to know what, if anything, the police had discovered at the shop or in the flat? And had there been any sign of a struggle or what?

'They went through the shop and the flat with a fine-tooth comb. Didn't find anything. Nothing. No signs of forced entry, nothing taken, no evidence of a struggle. Not a dickie-bird, old chap.'

'They got anything on where he was or what he was doing after the shop closed and before he was found in the morning?' asked Vince.

'Not yet. They're still checking it all out,' replied Wally.

Sid asked if they had any hunches, any leads?

'None that I'm aware of. It's completely baffling them down there. Total puzzlement,' Wally confessed.

'Mmmmh,' Vince sighed.

Sid turned again and thanked Wally. 'Leo here is going to give you some chips to play with downstairs, but *behave* yourself. Understand?'

Wally said in that greasy upper-class accent of his, 'I always do when I'm on your premises, Sid!'

'And make sure you do,' said Sid. 'And I want you to keep a strong watching brief on this. Anything you hear – anything at all – I want you giving us a bell right away. Got that?'

'Certainly, I will,' said Wally as Leo eased him through the doors and out the room.

When the doors had closed and the footsteps fallen away Sid whispered, 'Hear that, a .45 in the head?'

'We're dealing with someone or something that means business,' cautioned Vince.

'This is going to turn out to be some bad case of mistaken identity,' said Sid who was now shaking and looked as white as the stuff that used to arrive from South America in Jiffy bags addressed to Maria Aitkin.

Mistaken identity, eh?

Vince wasn't so sure.

'So what you got, Brian?' asked Sid as Lucksford sat down in one of the leather armchairs in the downstairs office.

'A bit of a thirst right now to tell you the truth,' replied the Chief-Super.

'Glass of Laphroaig?' asked Vince.

'That would do nicely, Vince,' said Lucksford as he helped himself to one of Sid's cheroots from the cabinet on the desk.

Sid lit a cheroot and put his feet up on the desk. 'We had old Wally here earlier. Got a bit of background from him, but not much. Not much at all really. What do you know?'

'I probably can't add much to what he said. It's early days yet in the investigation. They're still walking around in circles down there scratching their arses and hoping they'll stumble across something – thank you, Vince – so we'll have to wait and see what comes up, Sid.'

Sid wanted to know if they had made a connection with him yet?

Lucksford sipped the Scotch and thought for a moment. 'No, they haven't and there's no reason why they should. They know you're his brother, but they don't know who you are…and there's no reason why they should.'

'What about the CRO?' asked Vince.

'There's nothing in Criminal Records on you, Sid, apart from a couple of incidents of adolescent thievery. Nothing else.'

Sid wanted to know about the Organised Crime records.

'There's just the unsubstantiated stuff and the stuff from the odd grass that the collators have put together over the years, but the file is pretty moribund. Anyway, if the Margate lads had wanted to see the file I'd know about it. The application would go through my office.'

'Uh-huh,' Sid mumbled.

Vince was curious about the investigation. 'They got any theories yet? Any hunches?'

'As I said,' confided Lucksford, 'it's early days. They thought to begin with it might be robbery.'

Sid interrupted the Chief-Super, 'They didn't take the cash he had on him.'

'I know,' continued Lucksford, 'but it could have been. They might have been disturbed. Unlikely, but you don't know what went on. They've also considered it being a case of mistaken identity, but I think we can rule that out.'

'Why can we rule that out?' demanded Sid.

Lucksford looked at Vince and then back at Sid and said, 'Because, Sid, whoever did this was a professional, and those guys by and large make sure they get the right person. That's what they're paid to do. They can't afford to go around making mistakes.'

'Brian's got a point there, Sid,' added Vince.

Sid swung his feet off the walnut desk and paced up and down chomping on his cheroot, then he turned to Lucksford and said, 'You're telling me my brother was taken out by a professional hit man?'

'I'm not saying he was taken out by a professional hit man, I'm just saying whoever did it was someone who is used to this kind of work, someone with a hardened criminal background, that's all. It's obvious.'

Sid was digesting this when Vince asked if there were any other theories?

'They've got to keep an open mind. Another possible motive is revenge.'

'Revenge for what?' shouted Sid.

'They don't know. They're just keeping their options open,' said Lucksford.

Sid waved his cheroot and said quietly, 'Lionel never did anything wrong, never did anything that would result in *this*!'

'I know, but the Old Bill down there don't know that, do they?'

'That's true, Sid,' added Vince.

'We've just got to wait and see what happens with the investigation,' said Lucksford as he drained the cut-glass tumbler of the Islay malt. 'Just got to wait and see. There's nothing else we can do.'

Vince's Jaguar kept well within the speed limit as it proceeded up through Camden Town in the early hours of the morning. Somewhere far off there was a roll of thunder and then a flash of lightning.

'It's gonna rain,' said Sid who was sitting in the passenger seat.

'A hard rain's gonna fall,' noted Vince.

'What's that supposed to mean?'

'Nothing. It's from a song, isn't it?'

'No song I know,' stated Sid as he heaved the butt of his cheroot out the window.

Vince ignored the remark and said, 'We'll have you home before it starts pouring down, I hope.'

'Look, Vince, how about you staying up at the house tonight...perhaps a couple of days? I can rest a bit easier knowing you're about, you know?'

'Sure. Sid. If that's what you want.'

'Yeah, that's what I want.'

Sid and Vince enter the breakfast room at Sidiam and Sid tells Vince he's going to make them both the best nightcap he knows – Tia Maria in decaff coffee. 'You'll sleep like a judge.'

'Sounds OK by me.'

Vince presses the remote TV controller and channel hops the TV stations while Sid prepares the coffees.

'Who,' says Sid as he puts the two cups down on the table, 'have we got to fear? Just *supposing* this was a revenge killing or whatever *aimed at me*? Who?'

'Who we got to fear?' muses Vince as he sips the nightcap. 'Well, we've got, ultimately, the police, the judiciary, HM Customs, the VAT man, the Establishment, all the right-thinking citizens.'

'Yeah, but they don't go in for revenge killings, do they?'

'Let's hope they don't.'

'So who does that leave?'

'That's what I'm trying to figure out. All our enemies are either dead, compromised, or on our side now. I can't think of anyone who would pull this kind of stunt.'

'What about the Walker boys over in West London?'

'They're a vicious lot, but not stupid. They wouldn't do anything to rock the boat. They do their stuff and we do ours, you know?'

'Perhaps they're getting greedy? Think they can take over the whole show, know what I mean?'

'No way,' comforted Vince, 'they've got too much to lose.'

'So who've we got then?'

'There's nobody I can think of, Sid. The only person I'd put in the frame would be Simon Gould, but he's no longer with us.'

'No, he's keeping the crabs and mussels company down Clacton way, or what's left of him is. We took care of that one, didn't we? Eh? We took care of him!'

'Had to. A real threat to the fabric.'

'A right upper-class prick.'

'It could be,' says Vince as he finishes the coffee, 'that this is 100 per cent absolutely nothing to do with you. We still don't know.'

Vince didn't really believe that and neither did Sid.

Sid lay awake in bed as the storm broke and the rain cascaded down the windows. Who was out there who would do this to him? Who? Things had been quiet since... since Simon Gould – Sid could scarcely bring himself to say his name even now – since Simon Gould was sorted some ten years ago. He was a real threat for a couple of days, but Sid and the firm soon put paid to him and his mates. All of them. Put paid to them in spades.

Who else? Who else was a threat?

Peter Bell. He tried it on, didn't he? Didn't know what hit him, he didn't. Standing outside the Star Tavern in Belgravia carrying on and boasting and telling all those assholes that Sid was washed up? Standing there plotting his next move and then they pulled up and wound the windows down on the limo and pumped him full of more lead than the old shot tower on the South Bank had ever seen. That was a day to remember for Sid.

Tony Campisini. Now there was a little toe-rag of the first order, thought Sid. Tried to stir up some trouble with the South London lot and then play us off against each other and act as a double agent and then step in when it was all over! Huh! Phil wired up his Aston Martin over in Highbury and when Campisini turned on the ignition up it went. And him too, in a million pieces! Nothing of him left to bury. Somewhere Sid still had the video Phil shot of the explosion. Perhaps he'd dig it out and play it again? That would cheer him up.

Dennis the Dealer. There's another one. All those favours Sid did him and how did he repay him, eh? Got too greedy. Was going to murder Sid with the help of those two Italian geezers. Yes, murder Sid. Then take over the operation. Huh! Cyril gives the firm the word it's going to happen and Sid organises some dawn raids and then they've nabbed the three of them and before they know what's going on they're being fed into the furnace at a smelting works down Stratford way.

But that Simon Gould....

Sid was grooming him to be his number two, wasn't he? Treated him like a son. Had no secrets from him. Well, hardly any. He was going to run the operation so Sid could take early retirement – not that he'd ever really retire – and there was nothing Sid wouldn't do for him....

Turns out he was schmoozing the Gambiatti brothers from New Jersey behind Sid's back. Telling them Sid was past it and didn't have long to go and that he didn't command any loyalty or respect in London any more. And they almost believed him. Then he kidnaps Eric the Accountant and tortures him with a blow-torch for information on the hidden bank accounts and then he murders Joey and Del and tells me they've left the country and that's just for starters. He's stockpiling guns next and planning the coup and there he was sitting next to Sid each day and Sid doesn't suspect anything and Sid is wondering why he doesn't get calls back from New Jersey any more and why it looks like the American muscle and wherewithal ain't supporting him any more? And then, at the last fucking minute, the very last fucking minute before it all goes up, Phil walks in with this list of telephone numbers Simon has been dialling from his flat in Hyde Park Square and Sid sees he's been calling New Jersey night and day, talking to the Gambiatti brothers.

Phil said he has a nose for real villainy and he didn't think it was all kosher with our Simon but he needed proof before he said anything so he gets this list of numbers from some contact he's got in the telephone company and hands it over to Sid. At the last fucking minute!

If Phil wasn't a suspicious fucker, thinks Sid, I'd be enriching the rose beds out at Golders Green Crematorium now, wouldn't I? Eh?

Sid wants to get the full story so he pulls in Hector, Simon's buddy, and Phil gets to work on him and soon he's telling all he knows and spitting his teeth out at the same time. Sid does a blitz on all of Simon's other associates but he's fled the nest himself and then Sid and Phil get to work on the frightened faces and get a few leads and Phil and all the others are chasing about trying to find out where Simon is and meanwhile Sid is on the blower to New Jersey putting them right about this that and the other and ten thousand other things and saving the company's bacon and *that* wasn't easy. But Sid did it. And there ain't anyone else in this town that smart, Sid told himself.

And Simon himself, they tracked him down to that caravan in Essex…eventually. Thought he'd fled the country which was what he wanted Sid to think. Still plotting and planning right up until the end.

The caravan, yeah. Sid remembered it well. A couple of the lads went in first and shot Simon while he was sleeping. They put him in that body-bag, weighed it down with concrete, and Sid personally dumped him over the side and into Davy Jones' locker.

And that was the end of Simon Gould ten-odd years ago. At the bottom of the sea – him *and* his fucking Old Etonian accent, as Phil mused at the time.

Since then it's all been quiet.

But now this.

'It just ain't fucking good enough,' said Sid under his breath. 'Just ain't fucking good enough.'

2: Respects and Disrespects

THE FUNERAL CONVOY, as Leo called it, headed down the
M2 motorway towards Margate. Sid, Miriam, Vince and
Leo were in the Corniche with Harry at the wheel, and ahead
of them was the big Merc with Phil the Enforcer (driving)
and several other highly respected members of the firm.

Behind Sid were some six limousines full of those in the
company wishing to pay their last respects, and behind
them were five other limousines containing heads or repre-
sentatives of other firms who could not afford to be seen
ignoring the cremation of Sid's brother though none of
them had ever had the pleasure of the departed's company.

Sid was silent with a long face and Vince, Leo and Harry
took their cue from him. When the boss laughed, you
laughed. When the boss was depressed, you were depressed.

And keep it that way.

The only sound in the air-conditioned Corniche besides the ticking clock was Miriam's non-stop nineteen-to-the-dozen supercharged stream-of-consciousness monologue. The woman couldn't stop talking, about *this*, about *that*, about her feet, about a dented road sign, about her flight out to Miami in the afternoon from Gatwick (Phil was going to whiz her up immediately after the ceremony), about her new dress, about the stretch covers on the three-piece suite, and so on.

By the time the convoy had reached the bridge over the River Medway at Rochester, Sid had had enough. He cupped his hand over her mouth and screamed, 'Another peep out of you today and I'm tearing up those tickets to Miami! Got it?'

Miriam nodded understanding and Sid took his hand away.

'I was only going to say that — '

But Sid interrupted her. *'Button* it, right?'

She nodded again.

'Perhaps a spot of music on the radio, guv?' asked Harry.

There was no reply.

A few miles later Sid said, 'Lionel always wanted to be cremated, right?'

'Did he, guv? Fancy that! Never knew he wanted to be *cremated*,' said Harry.

'He did,' continued Sid, 'and you know what? The Old Bill said *No way*! Not until this investigation is over. He's *evidence*. We might need him. Imagine that, talking about Lionel as *evidence*! They said you can't cremate him until we say so, but you can bury him for the time being in case we have to dig him up. A bit fucking strong, ain't it?'

'It's what they always do, Sid, in cases like this,' said Vince.

'Yeah, but this is Lionel!'

'Don't make any difference,' replied Vince.

'Yeah, well…this is just *burying* him today. I'll give him a real send-off when I get the OK to cremate him. That's what he really wanted. Always said so, he did,' added Sid.

Miriam chipped in with the observation that 'I don't want to be cremated. Reminds me of the concentration camps.'

'Concentration camps! What do you know about concentration camps!? You weren't even born when they were on the go!' said Sid, turning on his wife.

'I know a lot about them, Sidney. My Auntie Sylvia was in one!'

'Yeah, look at her. Not even the fucking Gestapo could shut *her* up!'

Cemeteries are cemeteries. Vince didn't care for them whatever they were like. It wasn't the reminder of death that disturbed him, it was the constant harping on about the dead that got him. The English are never happier than when they are unhappy and moping and mourning around a cemetery was right up their street.

The rabbi was droning on and on and Vince had to prevent himself from falling asleep. He looked around the chapel at the impassive faces, most staring ahead, their eyes focused on infinity. Sid was at the front with tears streaming down his face. Miriam was next to him re-adjusting her lipstick with her tongue. Phil the Enforcer was scratching his nose. Leo was running his fingers up and down the creases in his trousers. Harry was staring out the window and running, no doubt, fantasies through his mind about retiring to a seaside cottage and opening a little garage....

And Vince. What was running through his mind?

Vince was thinking that somewhere out there, just beyond the limits of the cemetery, was someone who had the answers. Someone who knew what this was all about. Someone with an explanation, a reason and, perhaps, even, a justification.

And he was also thinking again about getting out of this game altogether and moving up to the Norfolk coast, to Wells-next-the-Sea....

The 'business' was soon over and then they were all kneeling down and praying for the departed.

Lionel was proud of his Jewish background. He was Orthodox, but not too Orthodox. Sid, however, had virtually disowned his Jewish background, didn't admit really to any of it. Didn't even generally acknowledge that his grandparents had fled Poland all those years ago during the pogroms. No, Sid had reinvented himself. He was his own creation. And he hoped he passed as a goy.

The sun temporarily shone for the burial which was, mercifully, short. Everyone stood around not knowing what to say and Vince was thinking that they might as well get used to it because they'd be back for the real thing one day, the cremation.

Ashes to ashes and dust to dust.

The next time around Sid will be able to take Lionel home with him. Resurrect him on the mantelpiece in a neat little box. Amen.

Miriam would just *love* that.

Everyone hung around for a while offering their condolences to Sid, then Phil drove off with Miriam to meet up with her sister at Gatwick for the Miami flight. The grey suits and the other firms got into their limos and heaved a big sigh of relief as they drove off and soon there was just Sid, Vince, Leo and Harry.

'I should've organised a wake or something for Lionel. He would have liked that,' said Sid as he wiped his nose.

Vince put his hand on Sid's shoulder.

'I never thought it would end like this,' Sid sobbed.

'I know. Why don't we all go for a drink and something to eat down the front?' suggested Harry.

Sid agreed. 'A good idea. Yeah. We'll go and have a drink, get a bite too.'

The Corniche pulled out of the gates of the cemetery and Sid gave Harry instructions as to which turnings to take through Margate.

Sid's route led them to a small road somewhere north of Cecil Square.

Harry was told to stop for a moment by Sid who pointed out the window at a slightly rundown neighbourhood newsagent's that declared itself to be BLATTNER'S.

Vince looked across. A small shop now bordered up on a modest early nineteenth-century terrace. So this was where the Blattner dynasty began. From small acorns....

'That window on the first floor *there*, that's the room where I was born. And then I had a bedroom up the top there I shared with Lionel. That's where I grew up...the first seventeen years of my life. That's where Lionel spent all his life. Never left the place....'

'I should pull forward, guv, we're blocking the street,' cautions Harry.

Sid hasn't heard him.

Vince nods at Harry to let him know it's OK to proceed.

The sound of sobbing fills the car.

Harry parks up the Corniche in the railway station fore-court, ensures the doors and the boot are firmly locked, gives a tenner to a railway porter to keep an eye on it, takes a couple of big deep breaths of seaside air, walks across the forecourt and down the approach, buys a postcard to send to his wife, and then ambles along the seafront in the direction of Marine Gardens to join the others in the restaurant....

'Fuckin' good this!' says Sid as he fills his mouth to capacity with a Hungarian chicken dish. Good, yeah, and the wine ain't too bad either. You having some, Vince?'

'No, guv. I don't like drinking when I'm on duty.'

'Have some!'

'No. I got a mineral water. I'm fine.'

'Your loss, son.'

The three men continued eating. Sid spoke about a couple of future deals they'd got coming up, Leo complained about the slowness of the solicitors in laundering money through their clients' account and told a joke about some lesbian going to a gynaecologist and him telling her that she had the cleanest vagina he'd ever seen and her replying, 'So it should be. I have a woman in twice a day', and Vince just stared across the small empty restaurant to the glass door and window.

Sid noticed this and said, 'Vince, you're not enjoying yourself. I'm the one in mourning, not you.'

Vince turned to Sid and said under his breath so that a passing waiter couldn't hear, 'There's something *wrong*.'

Sid and Leo realised then exactly what was wrong. Harry's dish which Sid had ordered on his behalf was stone cold and unstarted. If Harry wasn't sitting there it was because something had happened, because something had gone wrong. Harry was reliable, knew what the form was and never wandered off.

They knew not to question Vince when he said there was something wrong.

Vince patted the shoulder of his jacket and said to Leo, 'You didn't come out naked today, did you?'

'No, I didn't,' replied Leo.

'Good. Tell matey he's closing his restaurant now and get him to pull the blinds down and lock up front and back. Wait here. And don't do anything.'

Vince went through to the lavatories and pushed open the fire escape door he'd noticed when they had first arrived. He made sure the door was closed behind him and then stepped over the black bags and rubbish to a narrow alleyway that ran the length of the inclined terrace.

The alleyway was deserted apart from a large ginger cat cleaning itself some distance off. Down the hill was the direction to the station, and up the hill would take Vince to the beginning of the terrace up towards Cecil Square.

Vince went up the hill at a fast clip to where the alleyway joined a road that took him to the beginning of the terrace frontage. Nothing seemed out of order as he looked down, just the crowds, people milling about, nothing else.

He crossed to the sea side of the road and briskly walked down past the restaurant and towards the station. There was no sign of Harry, no sign of a disturbance or anything.

Down at the bottom of the hill Vince crossed to the Dreamland amusement park and checked out a couple of alleys and side streets. Nothing.

He walked over to the station and saw the Corniche parked up at the front. He looked around.

No trace of Harry.

Vince reached in his pocket for his mobile and called up Leo. 'How's everything?'

'Fine,' responded Leo, 'but there's no sign of Harry.'

'And there probably won't be.'

'Why's that?'

'I think he's ceased to be a player, that's why. Now, stay put while I get things organised. If anything happens, bell me.'

'Yeah.'

Vince retraced his steps back along the front, looking at faces, looking at vehicles, trying to find some clue or hint or suggestion of what had happened to Harry. The merry Margate life was continuing irrespective of whatever had become of their old mate.

Harry the Chauffeur had disappeared off the face of the earth somewhere between the station and the restaurant. A few hundred yards or so, enough for him to meet the Fates and vanish.

And nobody saw anything?

Leo shut his mobile phone, put it back in his top pocket and said, 'He's ready. We're to leave out the back.'

Sid got up and gave a roll of notes to the fat manager who was sitting shaking between his two cooks and a waiter. 'Thanks for the hospitality and this is for you to share out. Keep your mouths shut and you'll never hear from us again. Right?'

'Yes, sir.'

'Good.'

Sid followed Leo out to the lavatories.

'I'll go first,' said Leo as he gently pushed open the fire escape door with his left shoulder while holding his Glock pistol in his right hand. 'Uh-huh. All clear.'

They stepped over the rubbish in the yard and Leo peered up and down the alleyway. All clear again. They took a left up the hill to the corner where a guy in a red anorak and dark glasses started waving to them from the other side of the road. They soon realised it was Vince and he was standing by a VW Transporter he'd rented from Thanet-U-Drive.

Vince waved them in the back and started the engine as they pulled the side door closed behind them.

Sid wanted to know where the fucking Corniche was?

Vince said it was too risky going back for that right now. That could wait. He'd send Phil or someone down for it tomorrow or the day after when they knew the strength of it. The important thing now was to get out of Margate. Sid readily agreed.

Sid made himself comfortable on some foam and cardboard packing he'd found in the back. He felt safer there. Vince drove and Leo sat in the passenger seat with his Glock on his lap.

Vince pulled the VW off the motorway and into a service station near Ashford after reassuring Sid and Leo that they were definitely not being followed. Sid was desperate for a piss and Leo was desperate for a piss *and* something to drink.

They marched into the Gents together and marched out together and over to the counter where they got three coffees and three Danish pastries.

There was silence as they sipped their coffees until Sid said, 'You don't suppose Harry just had a heart attack or something as he was walking up the front? Had a funny turn? Could be in hospital right now. Got hit by a car?'

'If he did he'd show up in a hospital or something, but that, I think, is the last we'll ever hear of him...alive. He's gone. Someone's had him, I reckon. But I hope I'm wrong,' stated Vince.

Leo chipped in with, 'But we better check the hospitals and that tomorrow just in case.'

'Yeah, we will,' said Vince, 'but don't hold out any hopes. The mortuaries are where we should be checking.'

Sid was anxious about the welfare of Harry's wife should Harry prove to be no longer a living, breathing member of the firm. Vince said he'd go and see her, make sure she was OK, but she'd take it badly. Nothing much they could do except see she had no financial worries.

'How could he just vanish?' Sid wanted to know.

'Easy,' replied Vince, 'we've done it ourselves enough times. Somebody walks up to him with a gun under their coat, sticks it in his ribs and says, follow us, we want a little chat with you. Easy-peasy.'

'But Harry!' protested Sid. 'Our Harry!'

Vince finished his coffee and said, 'This was an opportunistic crime. Nobody could have planned it. They saw an opportunity and they grabbed it. Now, we can deduce from this that we were under surveillance from at least the moment we hit Margate, I think. They could have read about the funeral in the local paper. We can also deduce that whoever we're dealing with is very cautious and professional. They didn't try taking the three of us on, they only struck when they knew they'd succeed – when Harry was walking along the front alone.'

'So what does that tell us?' asked Sid.

Vince replied, 'That tells us whoever it is has to have a bit of respect.'

'RESPECT! I'm fucked if they're getting any respect from me!' yelled Sid at the top of his voice, disturbing the hubbub of the eatery.

After the rest of the clientele turned back to their plates

Vince said quietly, 'Sid, we're not dealing with a Spinksie here, you know.'

'Yeah, I know….'

The following day over breakfast Sid asked Vince what they should do about Edith, Harry's wife. 'Or should we do anything right now? I mean, perhaps we'll get a call from Harry today. Perhaps he just had some accident. There might be an innocent explanation for this.'

Vince buttered his croissant and ran the permutations through his mind and then said, 'She's used to him staying away, so let's not contact her just yet.'

'So what are we going to do? Check the hospitals down there, see if Harry's turned up? And the mortuaries and that?'

'We can't go phoning the local mortuary and asking if they've got a friend of ours staying there. We'd be setting off alarm bells. But I can check the hospitals,' said Vince as he finished his espresso. Then he added, 'Pity we've not got a copper on the payroll down there.'

'Yeah, Vince. You know, that's what we really need. Not just for Harry, but Lionel too. We need a nice contact in the police. Some copper who appreciates a little drink now and then. That's what we need. We need someone of ours on the inside. It's the only answer.'

'OK, then. We do exactly what we did with the Swansea business. We get Wallace off his big fat arse and we get him down there with some cover story and splashing out the spondulicks. He's got a nose for bent coppers like a pig has for truffles.'

'Right. He can tell them he's writing another one of his pot-boilers – *Seaside Crime*. They'll believe that. Sounds convincing, eh?'

'Yeah. Good one,' replied Vince.

'Where do you suppose the old fucker is right now?'

'In bed asleep.'

Sid punches out Wallace's home number on his mobile and it rings and rings until it is eventually answered.

'Wally? Good. It's *me*. Pack your toothbrush and grab a change of knickers...you're off to Margate for us...like fuck you are, Wally. You can knock that on the head right now. *You* do as you're *told*. I'll get hold of Perry and he'll pick you up in a couple of hours. I'll explain it all then. OK, sunshine? Out of bed and on your bike.' Sid pressed END on the handset and then while stuffing some toast into his mouth looked up at Vince and asked, 'Where's Perry now?'

'Collecting rents, I'd imagine.'

'Get him down to Wally's and we can get moving on this.'

'Got you.'

Vince phoned the hospitals down in Thanet that afternoon and they knew of no Harry Golding being admitted in the last twenty-four hours. Neither did they know of anyone meeting Harry's description. They didn't that day and they didn't the following day. Harry the Chauffeur had vanished. Whether he was at the bottom of the sea or mincemeat being served to pigs Vince didn't know, but Vince was sure that he would never be seen again.

Sid and Vince drove around to see Edith, Harry's wife, in Boreham Wood. A modest post-war council house in a cul-de-sac near what used to be a film studio. Luckily, her eldest daughter, Jacqui, was there for her to share her grief with. Sid assured her that he'd got a good pension plan for Harry and she'd have no financial worries, but what comfort was that to a woman who was denied even a body to bury?

Vince drove over to his small studio flat in Parliament Hill that evening to collect some clothes and things as Sid was still insisting he stay over at Sidiam. No sooner had he entered the flat and switched the TV on for the nine o'clock news than the mobile rings. It's good ol' Wally sounding as smug and self-satisfied as Jeffrey Archer on a chat show.

'Yeah, Wal?'

'I think I've rather done you two a favour.'

'Uh-huh.'

'I've got someone down there who's not averse to a drink and keeps his ear to the ground. His name's Terry Aveling.'

'What rank?'

'DS.'

'Good. You got his home number?'

'Sure have, old man.'

Vince took down the details.

'He's expecting a call...and he's very *thirsty*...is our Terry.'

'Did you ask him about Harry?'

'Well, you know the deal, no names, no packdrill. I didn't tell him anything about *that*. But no bodies have turned up, if that's what you mean.'

'That's what I mean. What about Lionel?'

'He knows about the investigation all right. Worked on it. But it was a little late in the evening and we'd had a drink or two too many, so you'll have to chat to him about that yourself.'

'OK,' said Vince.

'Now, remember, we scratch each other's backs here. If you come up with anything I want it first.'

'That's how we work.'

'Good.'

'And one other thing.'

'What's that, old chum?'

'Let Sid have your expenses and his change PDQ.'

'Not much change I'm afraid. We live in an expensive world.'

Don't I know it, thought Vince as he shut the phone off.

And where are my clean shirts?

They used to be here, I think.

But fuck them for the moment.

Vince decided he would relax for an hour with a bit of dope. Smoke a joint and listen to some jazz and chill out, as the kids now say.

He put on a Thelonious Monk CD and took out a three-paper joint from behind a brick in the fireplace (just one of several secret hiding places) and sat down in the armchair and took a couple of big hits straight off. If only Sid could see him now! He'd go apeshit. It was OK by Sid if you were an alcoholic but woe betide anyone in the firm who smoked a bit of grass! Sid couldn't differentiate between that and the hard drugs. He disapproved of all of it though he'd made a packet from distributing the stuff.

Fuck Sid.

Fuck the shirts too.

Get into the music. Get your head straight.

And remember, you don't have to spend the rest of your life working like this. You can change it. Get up to the Norfolk coast, to Wells….

But now it's just me – and Monk….

Sid was sitting on the leather couch in the downstairs back office at the club. He'd just come off the phone to a Norwegian businessman who had some very serious funny money in London he needed help in legitimising. Sid was the guy. Sid would see him next week and take care of it. And, it so happens, Sid had a new little venture in Great Yarmouth that would be the perfect venue for the dosh once it was deodorised: a couple of upfront amusement arcades with a little bit of the old coastal drug importing. This was all going to run smoothly, like a symphony, with everyone playing their part. Handsome it was.

Sid took a cheroot from the leather-covered box, lit it, looked up and said, 'Where was I?'

'You was going to explain about Margate, guv,' said Phil the Enforcer as he helped himself to a cheroot and offered the box to Leo who declined one.

'Don't be afraid to hand out the cheroots, lad,' said Sid with an irritated edge to his voice, 'and perhaps Vince would like one too?'

Phil went to offer the box to Vince and then twigged

that Sid was taking the piss. 'Erh, sorry, guv.'

'I don't mind you having one, Phil, but how about waiting for me to offer you one, eh? It's called good manners. Know about that?'

'Yeah, I'm with you.'

'That's all right then,' continued Sid, 'and now, Vince here, he's told you about the copper down in Margate and he's given you his number. Right?'

'Right,' say Leo and Phil in unison.

'Right. So the idea is as nobody else seems to be getting anywhere investigating Lionel's death and Harry's disappearance we're going to do it ourselves. I don't care what it takes as long as I get answers. You two are going down there and you're going to turn that poxy seaside resort upside down and resolve this aggro. Keep in regular touch with Vince and let him know anything that happens. Got it?'

'Got it,' said Phil.

'Got it,' said Leo.

Sid looks across at Vince and says, 'You got anything to add?'

'Not much,' says Vince and then, turning to Phil and Leo, 'You two know how to handle yourselves. Be discreet and keep a low profile – you know how bad publicity and trouble is for us. Make sure nothing can be traced back here.'

'Consider us there,' says Phil.

3: The Walls Have Hearsay

THE FOLLOWING DAY Vince drove Sid out to Heathrow and there they caught a plane up to Newcastle for an afternoon meet with the three Halliday brothers who wanted some interim financing for a leisure complex they were developing out at Wallsend. Sid liked the proposals and the deal was agreed on the spot. A couple of hours later, after drinks and a meal, Vince and Sid were flying back to London.

Sid's phone rings while Vince is doing over the limit on the motorway somewhere west of Isleworth. It's Danny Hope, the arch creep (in Vince's estimation) and onetime 1960s pop star who always fancied himself as an all-round entertainer but now also fancies himself as an entrepreneur. As Vince once said of him, 'He's got a mobile phone and a Filofax and all he needs now is a bright idea.'

'Sid, we've got to meet,' says Danny.

'Oh, yeah. My days of record plugging are over, son,' says Sid who then laughs with Vince at the remark.

'No. Serious. Your brother and Harry. I think I know who's behind it. We need to meet.'

'Harry, eh? Word gets about fast.'

'We got to meet, Sid. I'm serious.'

'You got something you got to tell us then?'

'That's right.'

'Where you now?'

'At home.'

'Stay put. We'll be there shortly.'

Sid closes the phone and says to Vince, 'Call by Danny boy's place. He's got something to tell us. Thinks he knows who's behind it.'

'He does?' says Vince incredulously.

'That's what he says.'

'That short-arse has never been privy to anything.'

'You never know.'

Vince pulled the Merc up outside Danny's London house, a mews cottage in the crotch of Cromwell and Earls Court roads. Danny saw them arrive from upstairs and hurried down to open the front door. He was agitated and worried and looked like he could do with another Valium or two. They followed him up the stairs past dozens of framed photographs of himself taken in the early 1960s and into the main room, again festooned with photographs of himself, all from the same period.

Danny sat down in the middle of a leather-and-chrome sofa and immediately started rabbiting on about some company he'd just bought into that manufactured fireworks for the Saudis.

Sid looked at Vince, cleared his throat, and said, 'I've heard all this guff before. Spare us, Danny.'

'Of course,' Danny replied, before launching into some rambling dialogue about how he's got a new TV series coming up where he plays the only merchant banker in the City from a working-class background.

'Danny!' shouted Sid, 'you're wasting my fucking time! *Wasting* it!'

'I'm sorry,' stutters yesterday's idol.

'Tell me what I've come to hear. OK!'

Vince remembered what Phil the Enforcer had once said about Danny. That he probably went to bed at night with a rubber doll of himself. Vince chuckled.

Danny turned quickly and glared at Vince and then looked back at Sid, 'What's he laughing at?'

Sid leant forward until his face was only about six inches from Danny's and said quietly, 'Vince has a sick sense of humour. He's probably laughing at all the things he's going to do to you if you continue wasting our time.'

Danny blanched, closed his eyes and said he needed a drink.

'Fuck the drink. Start talking!' Sid ordered.

'OK. I got a bit worried when I heard about your brother…what with you and me having a few dealings and so on. I thought to myself, if Sid Blattner goes down I'm going to go down too.'

'Wipe that out of your head. I'm not going anywhere, Danny.'

'Yes, of course. I didn't mean that…not *that*. Know what I mean…as it were.'

No wonder he's known as Arse-Squeak behind his back, thought Vince.

'Anyway, I was more than a bit worried,' continued Danny, 'and I was down at the Flamingo over the weekend and talking to some of the local faces and I got talking to this geezer, Mel Kelly.'

Vince thought the name rang a bell. 'Where's matey from?'

'Edmonton,' said Danny.

'Uh-huh,' acknowledged Vince.

Sid looked up at Vince. 'We know him?'

'Yeah, we do. His real name is Mendel Levy.'

'*Him*? The fur trade fraudster who went down over that charity scam?' asked Sid.

Vince replied, 'The same.'

'Huh. Now get on with the story, Danny boy.'

'Sure, Sid. Well, we were having a few drinks and I said I often saw you at charity dinners and fund-raising events and that – but I didn't tell him anything else! – and he said I was wasting my time associating with you as you weren't going to be about much longer.'

Sid asked with disbelief, 'Pray tell, why's fucking that?'

'Because Ray Seago's got it in for you and he's taking over your empire. That's what he said.'

'When did you hear this?'

'About a fortnight ago. I didn't pay too much attention… but then, you know, all *this* happened….'

Ray Seago?

The Merc is stuck in a traffic jam at Hyde Park Corner.

Sid is banging the dashboard with his fist. 'That fucking Ray Seago! I might have known it. I might have known it! He's been too fucking quiet lately and now we know why. Why didn't I realise, eh?'

'We don't know anything for sure yet. It's just gossip,' Vince cautioned.

Sid ignored Vince. 'Why didn't *I* realise? We should have put paid to that fucker back in 1985 when he opened that club in Ilford. None of this would have happened now. None of it.'

'Sid, we don't know.'

'Sure we do. It's him all right. Sneaky little bastard. Well, he's going to get his comeuppance this time all right – in fucking spades. I'll see to that.'

Vince clamped his hand on Sid's shoulder and said, 'We don't know anything yet, we've just got tittle-tattle from Arse-Squeak, that's all. We've got to be cool and cautious.'

'So what do we do?'

'Let's get the scumbag furrier in and see what he's got to say about it.'

'Better than that, we'll go mob-handed over to Seago's place and settle it there and then.'

'What if we're wrong?'

'We're not, are we?'

'We don't know, Sid. Look, I think Seago is a chancer and he'll do anything he thinks he can get away with, but I don't think he'd do this. He's been running his own little operations up in Essex with all the other little Essex lads and he doesn't want trouble. We haven't heard a peep out of him in years.'

'No, because he's been plotting. That's why. Anyway, we remove him and what have we got to fear?'

'Nothing from him but he's got a lot of little allies and if they all got the hump with us it wouldn't be our downfall, but we'd end up with some lingering headaches. You with me?'

'I'll get fucking Mendel Levy picked up then. Who'll we send?'

'Rufus and Winston.'

'Yeah, he can't bear the blacks, can he?'

Mendel Levy was halfway through a salt-beef sandwich and halfway through a porno video in the office out the back of Mendel Furriers, just down the road from Bloom's restaurant in Golders Green Road, when Sylvia the manageress knocked, pushed the door ajar, and said, 'Mr Levy, two *shvartzers* are here to see you.'

'Me?' said Mendel. 'For them, what can *I* do?'

'They've come from Mr Blattner.'

'Jesus Christ! Tell them I'm not here. I'm gone!'

As Mendel got to his feet and crammed the remainder of the sandwich in his mouth Sylvia was pushed into the room by Rufus and Winston. She fell to the floor and screamed. Rufus took Mendel by the arm and said, 'You're coming down to Dalston with us, Jew-boy.'

'That's right, bro,' added Winston. 'We're going for a ride.'

Rufus pushed Mendel into Winston's arms and knelt down beside Sylvia and said in a whisper, 'Any peeps from you, mama, an' black man's gonna come back an' bludgeon you with his big hard-on!'

Sylvia found the idea rather appealing.

Mendel was shouting and screaming as Rufus and Winston dragged him into the upstairs boardroom at Albion Non-Ferrous Metals (1947) Ltd in Dalston.

Winston gave him a whack across the face with the back of his hand and that shut him up a while, certainly long enough for them to tie him, hands and ankles, in the 'interrogation chair' as it was known.

'Now,' said Rufus, 'Mr Blattner'll be by in his own time later this evening an' he's got some questions for you. So you better have some answers, otherwise his boys'll start work on you while we pay a visit to your cute little wifey an' I bet she ain't ever had two of the brothers at the same time, eh?'

Then Rufus secured a gag around Mendel's mouth with gaffer tape.

Winston being the last one out the room had the courtesy to switch the light off, leaving Mendel awash in moonlight and high anxiety.

It was about four hours later in the early hours of the morning when Sid, Vince and Ron the Doorman from the club arrived in Dalston. Mendel had pissed himself a couple of times, looked as white as a sheet and had eyes redder than the setting sun.

Sid pulled the gaffer tape off him and Mendel let out a yell that echoed throughout the empty room.

Mendel was glad to see them. He was glad to see anyone.

'Sid has got a couple of questions for you, Mendel,' said Vince. 'Answer them promptly and succinctly. Right?'

Mendel nodded his head in horrified agreement and

said, 'I haven't done anything. Anything at all. Nothing!'

Sid took a couple of steps towards Mendel, paused, stared him in the eyes and stated, 'We saw our old friend Danny Hope recently. He tells us that you told him Ray Seago had it in for me and that I wasn't going to be about much longer? That true?'

'I'll tell you what happened. I took the wife out to that night-club in Colchester he, Ray, runs – Tiberius' Hideaway. Know it?'

Sid nods.

'It was a night out for me and the wife and I thought I might get some business out of Ray because his wife's had a couple of minks out of me before, few years ago, you know? Just a bit of business. That's all. Ray didn't turn up after all but there were some of the other Essex lads there, real loudmouths. I said I'd sold *your* wife a mink coat and they were a bit pissed and they said – who the fuck is Sid Blattner? And I told them who you were and they said if you ever set foot in Essex they'd have you for breakfast. Just bragging and that. That's all. Real loudmouths. I saw Danny a few days later and I just said to him that Ray had some real rough lads on his patch and it might not be a safe place for you to visit. Nothing else. That's all.'

'Danny tells us that you told him Ray was planning to take me and the operation over.'

'You know what Danny's like, Sid. His mouth outraces his brain. He puts his own spin on everything. He can get six out of two and two. You know that.'

'When did you last see Ray then?'

'Two years ago about.'

'When did you last speak to him?'

'A few weeks ago before we went up to Colchester.'

'Did you phone him or did he phone you?'

'I phoned him.'

'Why?'

'I had a few new minks in, I told you. They were moving slowly. I wanted to shift them.'

'Uh-huh.'

'He sounded funny.'

'How funny? Telling jokes or what?'

'I don't know…just funny. Like his mind was some-where else.'

Sid looked at Vince and Vince knew exactly what Sid was thinking: his mind was somewhere else because he was plotting against *me*, Sid Blattner. That wasn't Vince's interpretation necessarily, but don't disagree at this stage of the game.

'So, you goes up there, Mendel, and Ray doesn't show. Right?'

'Right, Sid. He didn't show.'

'End of story?'

'End of story.'

'OK. Now you've done me a real favour coming down here in your own time and sharing your knowledge with us. I appreciate it. And I owe you one.'

'Thanks, Sid. Any time.'

'Ron, chauffeur Mr Levy back home.'

'Sure, guv.'

'Come on, Vince. We got business to do.'

Vince nods at Mendel and follows Sid out of the room and down the corridor.

There was nobody across in Essex who could give Sid the inside track. Not any more. Fuck it, he thought, who can I ask? Who'd know what was going on in that god-forsaken stretch of useless real estate?

The greasy-spoon café that Morris Peltz ran in Archer Street hadn't changed since the mid-1950s – the same uncomfortable chairs, Formica-covered surfaces, tea urns, cups and saucers even, or so it seemed to Sid. But he liked it that way. It reminded him of his early days 'up West', here in Soho, soon after he arrived from Margate and was scampering around on the make. Not only that, everyone in the café seemed to have something to hide and it was therefore a good place to meet. All the other faces were too busy worrying about what *they* had to keep secret to worry about what *you* had to keep secret.

Vince sipped his tea and pulled a face. It was bitter and tasteless at the same time. Sid noticed and said, 'Morris here'll never be able to make a decent cup of tea or coffee as long as he's got a hole in his arse.'

Sitting opposite Sid and Vince was Benny Kravitz, a Boris Karloff lookalike in his early seventies with deep-set eyes and a face that was always bereft of emotion. It wasn't so much Benny's face as the enormous grey overcoat he was wearing that caught Vince's attention. Enormous in every way – vast, wide lapels, buttons as big as hubcaps, ankle-length, and heavy. Vince wondered if it had been bought in the 1930s, and he was right.

Sid pushed his empty cup forward on the table and in an uncharacteristically reverential tone said, 'Benny, I need your help on something.'

Benny said nothing.

'We're having more than a little *bother* right now,' continued Sid, '...and we don't know what...uh...*quarter* it's coming from.'

Benny lit an untipped cigarette with a heavy, gold lighter that had his initials engraved on the side.

Vince picked up the thread. 'We've heard some rumours that Ray Seago might be behind it. That he might be planning to write Sid out of it, take over the operations.'

Benny nodded and from lips that hardly moved said, 'And?' in a voice with the resonance of a Thames tug.

'*And*,' whispered Sid, 'we were wondering if you'd... uh... heard anything?'

Benny shook his head from side to side. 'I've heard nothing, but then Benny doesn't always hear everything these days. My good friend Harry Solomons retired out there on the coast, he'd know, but he passed away last month.'

'So you've heard nothing?' asked Sid.

'Nothing,' continued Benny, 'and neither have I heard anything from elsewhere. Who do *you* think is behind this?'

'The only name we got in the frame,' said Sid, 'is Ray Seago. There's nobody else.'

Benny leant forward and stated, 'Ray Seago could have been a threat a few years ago when he was hungry, but I don't think so now. He's got flabby. Your problem is elsewhere.'

'Where elsewhere?' asked Sid.

'I don't know. Just elsewhere. A feeling, you know?' replied Benny in a lugubrious tone.

Sid was startled by this statement. 'Then why they doing it?'

Benny took another cigarette from his silver cigarette case, lit it up and sighed when he realised he already had one on the go in the ashtray.

'What's your counsel on this then?' asked Vince.

'Be vigilant,' responded Benny. 'There's nothing else I can tell you.'

Vince arrived back in his studio flat just after midnight. He put the coffee percolator on and noticed a note fixed to the door of the fridge with a magnet and written in caps:

> TOO MUCH TROUBLE TO PHONE?
> I CAN'T WAIT ABOUT ANY LONGER.
> GIVE ME A CALL WHEN YOU'RE
> BACK IN THE REAL WORLD.
> – Lisa

He read the note a couple of times and sighed loudly and deeply. He looked at the black-and-white photo of Lisa pinned to the cork noticeboard by the window and sighed again. A good looking girl, but not easy to live with. Not that Vince really lived with her. She semi-moved in about six months ago and that was when the strains and tensions of the relationship began to surface. But even so....

From the back of a drawer he took out a package wrapped in silver paper. He unfurled the paper and removed a pre-rolled joint about five inches long. Vince lit the joint and took a couple of hits and wandered through to the main room where he switched on the CD player.

As Charlie Parker's *Anthropology* leaps out of the speakers Vince falls on the sofa and takes a few more hits. He's feeling really mellow and he's feeling at one with the music.

Then the telephone rings.

Vince lazily reaches out and picks up the receiver.

'Uh-huh?'

'Vince? It's Phil.'

'How's it going, man?'

'Fine. You doing wacky dust or something?'

'No, just a bit of reefer madness.'

They both laugh.

Phil says, 'I didn't want to phone you at Sid's. I thought it better I spoke to you at home. We can talk more freely.'

'Good thinking, pal. What you come up with?'

'Not a lot. We've seen that lady who worked for Lionel and his few friends. They're all clapped-out geriatrics who play bowls and stuff. There's nothing there. They're as innocent as a nun's pussy. Didn't seem to have an enemy in the world down here.'

'Uh-huh. How about the copper?'

'He's a funny piece of work all right. On the take. Fancies himself a lot.'

'What's he say?'

'Not a lot. The investigation floundered. They had nothing to go on and didn't know where to take it. But two things came up of interest.

'Apparently they found this powder on old Lionel's clothes. Dye it was. And there's this old abandoned dye works down here somewhere and they think he was taken there and shot before being dumped on the beach.'

Vince said, 'That's interesting. You going to check it out?'

'Yeah, top of the list,' replied Phil. 'And the other thing they came up with was this – old Lionel was a real regular at this massage parlour on…here it is…Northdown Road.'

'He liked his wand massaged then?'

'Yeah. Seems so, but this may have nothing to do with what happened to him.'

'That's true. Keep it to yourself. It's probably irrelevant. It would only upset Sid.'

'That's what I thought. Caesar's Massage Parlour! The names they come up with down here. It's run by some ageing Judy, name's Vicky Brown. I had a chat with her.'

'Anything kinky about him?'

'No, just straight hand-jobs, she reckons. She didn't really know. Some young tart was always on his case, name of Candy Green, occasional worker there. He didn't want it with anyone else.'

'You seen this Candy bint?'

'Not yet. About here somewhere but a bit elusive, you know?'

'*You* getting any down there?'

'Only your sister.'

'Not my mother?'

'*Ciao.*'

'*Ciao.*'

Vince took a couple more hits, closed his eyes and sailed off to sleep with *A Night in Tunisia*. An hour later the smell of a burnt-out coffee percolator would wake him up.

'So they've come up with nothing so far?' said Sid to Vince as they turned into Wardour Street and walked south through Soho.

'The dye works is a lead. Phil's looking into that,' replied Vince turning up the collar of his jacket as a light rain half-heartedly began to fall.

'Not much, is it?'

'They're digging.'

'What are the Old Bill thinking, motive-wise?'

'They're stumped. Don't know. They've been playing around with the idea that it was a case of mistaken identity.'

Sid stopped and turned to Vince. 'We all entertained that idea, didn't we? And then when Harry disappeared it went out the window.'

'You're right, Sid.'

'Tell them down there I want to see some action on this. And fast.'

'They're doing all they can.'

'Look, there's a fucking cab! Oi, cab!'

Sid waved the cab down, barked an instruction for the club over Curzon Street way to the cabby and climbed in. Vince followed him.

'Now,' says Sid, 'the other little item on the agenda I want some action fast on is that prick out in Essex, Ray Seago. We've got to move on that and find out what's going on.'

Vince looked puzzled. 'What you got in mind? Not that we know for sure he's got anything to do with it.'

'My idea is this. I give him a bell and say why don't we meet up? I got a little business venture for you, Ray, and it's just up your street.'

'So, he turns up for a meet. Then what?'

'Low key to begin with. I put up some scheme and I can tell by the way he behaves and reacts whether he's up to some skulduggery. I can read him. I can read most people.'

'Then what?'

'We get heavy and beat the fucking shit out of him and show him who runs things around here and then he gets fed to the fish downstream. He won't understand anything else.'

Vince frowned. 'That's how we're going to do it?'

'You got a better way?'

'He's not going to turn up for a meet on his lonesome.'

'I'll have double whatever he turns up with. This little cocksucker is a blight on the face of God's earth. We're doing society a favour getting rid of him.'

Vince knew that things were never that simple.

Sid's sitting in the back office at the casino eating a steak sandwich and eyeing over a balance sheet. 'Good figures, here, Vince. Good figures.'

'Mario's got some good figures too here.'

Sid looks up. 'You know, you're right. Those croupiers Ernie Issacs used to get all looked like someone's sister, didn't they? But the girls Mario gets – pretty fucking serious, eh? Each one a cutie. A real cutie.'

'Lifts the tone of the whole place.'

'Sure does...anyway, let's phone this arsehole out in Essex and put Operation *Götterdämmerung* into first gear. You got his new number?'

Vince passes a blue Post-It note across the desk.

Sid's eyes glint in the half-light of the office. 'This is the beginning of the end for *Mr* Ray Seago.'

Sid presses the buttons on the touch-tone phone with all the seriousness and determination of a lion closing in for a kill. 'Come on Ray, baby, say your prayers.'

The phone rings at the other end and a male voice answers.

'Hello...Ray? It's Sid, Sid Blattner...oh, yeah, I see... when will he be back? Uh-huh...you don't know...*they* don't know...when was this? I am sorry...yes...perhaps I'll visit him...yes...thank you.'

Sid returns the handset to the cradle and writes something on the jotter.

Vince is curious. 'What's going on?'

'That was his son.'

'Uh-huh?'

'Seems Ray has been hospital for the last few weeks. With depression.'

'Depression?'

'Yeah, he's in some private loony bin out Dunmow way.'

'Does he sound on the level?'

'I don't know. This could all be a bit of a ruse to throw us off the scent.'

'We better get it checked out.'

'Better than that, we'll check it out ourselves. I got the name of the place here.'

Vince turned the Corniche off the A120 just to the west of Dunmow and headed up a country lane in the direction of Broxted (according to the road sign). It was a bright day but cold.

Sid was sitting in the back with Kenny and Nathan and in the front passenger seat was Mickey. This was the firm's heavy gang, the heavies who were brought out for special occasions, the faces who didn't need to be told what to do in the event of things going rotten. A triumvirate of Hard Men all tooled up and ready to go, and all kitted out in Hugo Boss jackets that looked as if they belonged to someone else.

'Here we are,' said Vince as he turned into the drive of the Glebe Grange Nursing Home. Ahead was the large house itself, standing in isolated splendour and probably dating back to the middle years of the last century. All was quiet and nobody was to be seen.

'Eerie place this,' said Sid.

'Good job nobody's expecting us,' stated Nathan. 'We'd be handicapped all right.'

Vince pulled up in front of the main entrance and stopped the engine. The Hard Men got out one at a time, each eyeing the buildings and the grounds. Then Vince got out and, finally, Sid who strode up the sandstone stairs. Kenny and Nathan entered the home first and then waved the others in.

The main reception hall was tastefully and expensively furnished but the smell of antiseptic that lingered in the air was a constant reminder that this place wasn't somewhere you came to have a good time.

A young nurse appeared and asked if she could be of help? Sid said he'd come to visit an old friend. Did Sid have an appointment? No. Well, in that case, she'd have to fetch Sister and he'd have to speak to *her*.

Sister soon appeared, a stout woman in her late forties with red hair. Her manner was pleasant and kindly. 'I'm Sister Reaney. I understand you've come to see a friend and you *don't* have an appointment?'

'Yes. I'm Sidney Blattner and I'm an old friend of Ray Seago's.'

'Mr Seago, yes. I see.'

'We were in the area and we just thought we'd pop in an' that.'

'Uh-huh.'

'Perhaps you can tell him we're here? If anyone can cheer him up it's us.'

'I'm afraid it would take a lot more than that to cheer him up,' said the sister.

'It would?'

'Uh-huh. Mr Seago is suffering from a very severe depression.'

'Can we see him? We'll cheer him up, won't we lads?'

Ray Seago's face was leached of all colour. There was a grey pallor about him that made both Vince and Sid feel uneasy. His eyes were dark and sunken, staring ahead, focused on infinity, dampened by tears. Inside his head was the burden of all humanity's sadness and suffering.

'Ray, it's me, Sid. I've brought you some flowers.'

No tremor of recognition or emotion danced across Seago's face. He just sat there, propped up in bed, out of touch with everything except his own inward churning torments.

Vince looked up and said, 'How long he been like this then?'

The sister said, 'On and off for two years now. He gets a little better sometimes and we let him go home, and then a few weeks later he's back.'

'Why's he like this?' asked Sid.

'If we knew the answer to that we'd have a cure,' whispered the sister softly.

'Can't you give him something?' Sid continued.

'We have....'

Sid and Vince thanked the sister and hurriedly left the room to join the three others outside in the corridor.

'So what's the deal?' said Nathan.

'We drive back to London. The show's over today,' stated Sid.

'Over?' echoed Nathan.

Vince and Sid exchanged glances and each knew exactly what the other was thinking. 'Don't say it,' said Sid, 'I know. He ain't behind anything.The only thing he could be behind in is his mortgage payments.'

Phil peered out from behind the stack of old 50-gallon drums and looked up along the derelict railway track towards the dye works. There, just *there*. Movement. The stocky figure in blue denims with the blond hair, there in the shadows, entering the building through that side door? It was movement all right, but was it him? It was something. It must have been him. Must have. What else could it have been? He's nowhere else.

Phil looked over his shoulder back the way he had come, down towards the rusty marshalling yard circum-scribed with a high security fence and the backs of some old terraced houses. Not there. Must be *here*.

A smell of decay and abandonment. The world's moved on. An odour too of festering oil and noxious liquids from the drums, seeping and leaking on to the ground that was here as bereft of plant and insect life as a marble slab. Phil wondered what was in these containers and how was it that they could just be dumped here and left to rot?

There's another smell here too that Phil begins to notice – death. He can taste it on his tongue too. Of deaths past? Of deaths future? Of deaths present? He did not know, but it lingered there at the tip of his tongue, an unwelcome presence.

Movement again!

There, behind that glassless window on the ground floor in the corner. Something moved, just briefly. A rearrangement of shadows for a fleeting moment of time gave the game away. He's there.

Phil took the Smith and Wesson revolver out of his shoulder holster, checked it was fully loaded and then released the safety catch. Clasping it in his right hand he moved back along the drums to a small train shed built of blue engineering bricks. The wooden doors of the shed were rotted and half off their hinges. Phil managed to prise them apart far enough for his slim figure to enter.

Most of the roof had caved in and the light that came through allowed Phil to pick his way safely through the debris and rubble to the front of the shed where he crouched behind the one remaining door.

He had a clearer view of the empty factory now. It was three storeys high and built of stock red brick. It was a hundred or more years old. There wasn't a sheet of glass left in the place. Plants grew out of the brickwork and bracken sprouted from downpipes and hopper heads. The white decorative lettering between the first and second floors was still readable: PRESCOTT & FORSTER'S THANET DYE WORKS.

Somewhere in there is this arsehole, thought Phil, and when I get him I'm going to get some answers. This little business is in imminent danger of being wrapped up, and Symphony Sid is going to be well pleased...and over the moon. I'll get him some answers.

But first....

Phil moved back through the train shed and out through the gap at the other end. Cautiously he then looked around the corner of the shed to the dye works – there was no movement, no noise, no nothing. The scene looked as lifeless and still as a bad snapshot.

The only way Phil could see to get to the dye works was down the side of the shed where he would be hidden and then sprint across the yard where he wouldn't be hidden.

The yard was about twenty yards wide and Phil figured that if he did it quietly and nobody was looking out of a window as he sped across he'd make it safely. The other factor, of course, was that Mr Denim can't know he's being followed and therefore his vigilance isn't what it should be.

No ifs, ands or buts, thought Phil. This is the only way to do it.

He moved down the side of the shed and paused at the end as he looked around and across. No noise, no movement, no nothing. Time to do it.

Phil raced across the yard on his toes making not a sound and reached the factory. He pressed his back against the wall and waited to see if anyone had been alerted. There was just silence. Heavy lingering silence.

Showtime coming up, thought Phil as he raised the S&W revolver.

Let's get moving.

Sid walked back into the lounge at Sidiam in a silk dressing gown holding two bottles of lager, one of which he gave to Vince who was spread out on the sofa watching a football game on a satellite station.

'What's the match?' asked Sid.

'No idea,' said Vince.

'Aren't you watching it?'

'Yes, but the commentary's in Spanish or something.'

'Uh-huh.'

Vince took a mouthful from the bottle while Sid lit a cheroot and made himself comfortable in an armchair.

'Well, that was a waste of a fucking afternoon, wasn't it? Travelling up there to Essex,' said Sid as he reached forward for the TV controller and began channel hopping.

Vince took another swig. 'Not at all. We established that poor old Ray *isn't* the guy we've got to worry about.'

'Suppose that's true. What do we do now then? And what are those two wankers getting up to down there in Margate? They come up with anything yet?'

'Let's give them a bell and see.'

Vince took his slim notebook out of an inside jacket pocket and flicked through the pages. 'Here we are. The Cozy Towers, some bed-and-breakfast place.'

While Sid was chomping on his cheroot Vince dialled up the number. It started ringing and it continued ringing and ringing.

'They got a b&b place where nobody answers the fucking phone? Eh?' hissed Sid.

'Somebody should answer. Give it a jiff.'

'I'll dial it again. I might have mis-dialled.'

'Yeah.'

The number continued ringing...

...at the Cozy Towers b&b hotel where the telephone is situated on the wall just down from the front door in the reception area of the passage.

The phone continues ringing and the sound resonates through to the kitchen and up the stairs to the first landing.

The front door bangs open and closed in the strong wind that now comes in off the Channel. A small grey cat peers into the corridor and then hurriedly darts away as the door begins to close.

Mrs Peggy Hatchard, the landlady, in normal circumstances, would have answered the phone, but today's circumstances were for her decidedly not normal: she was on the floor of the sitting room with two bullet holes in her chest, dead.

In the adjoining dining room two middle-aged guests, a husband and wife, both in their sixties and from Leamington Spa, also lay dead from gunshot wounds.

On the first floor in the No. 2 back bedroom Leo lies on his back, motionless and staring at the ceiling. Red-tinged foam trickles from his mouth. He's gone to sleep permanently, with a bullet hole in his head.

Now the blue of twilight is turning to night's black as Phil edges along the wall of the first floor of the dye works. His heart is beating like a Gene Krupa single stroke drum roll and a patina of icy perspiration covers his face, chest and arms.

It didn't quite work out how Phil thought it would.

He realised this when he got up the stairs, but by then he was in the web and trapped. He'd been lured here. This was all part of the plan. The burst of semi-silenced semi-automatic fire caught him by surprise. He fell to the floor and realised then that they meant business every bit as seriously as he did.

Those heavy footsteps that suddenly stopped. I know they're here. They know I'm here.

How many there were exactly Phil didn't know. There could be two or three or even just the one. He had no way of knowing. All he could do was just move along silently and wait for them to make a move, hope they'd slip and make a sound and give their position away.

They're out there somewhere in the darkness, but where?

Phil reached a window. He fell to his hands and knees and slowly and quietly moved underneath it.

There was a sound above him, or was it in front of him? Somebody moving.

Phil remained motionless, waiting to hear it again. Afraid to move.

He waited and waited, for what seemed like hours. Every second crushing down upon him.

Nothing else. Just silence.

There's someone out there, that's for sure.

But, for Chrissakes, *where*?

If only he'd insisted Leo had come along with him. Things would have been so much easier. The two of them together could have soon taken care of this little niggling problem. No mistake. Taken care of it right away.

It's too late to start getting regretful. The problem has got to be faced as it is now.

Yeah.

I've been in worse situations before and I've always got out of them. I'm a resourceful guy when the chips are down…but *I* can count on *me*. I've got myself out of other fixes and this is going to be no exception.

And another noise. Coming from over there, from the stairs silhouetted against the night sky. Somebody's stumbled on something. I know where they are. I fucking know where they are!

Silence again. Hard penetrating silence that almost bursts your eardrums.

Just wait another moment and then spring up and make for the stairs.

You'll nail him all right, Phil, old boy.

But then the phone rang.

Phil's mobile phone.

The sharp, insistent electronic burble echoed throughout the first floor.

As Phil fumbled for the Nokia handset in his jacket pocket a rake of semi-auto fire cut through the gloom and while only two of the twelve bullets hit Phil that was enough for his life to be terminated there and then.

The phone continued ringing for a couple of minutes until a hand that was not Phil's opened it and shut the power off.

Once again the dye works was enveloped in silence.

'It doesn't look like Phil's answering right now,' observed Vince as he replaced the phone on the cradle. 'Perhaps he left it at the hotel and went out on the town?'

Sid was furious and banged the empty bottle of lager down on the glass-topped coffee table. 'I send these two wankers down there and I can't even get hold of them to find out what's going on! I mean, what is this? Eh? It pisses me off.'

'I'll try them again later,' said Vince tentatively.

'Yeah, and you tell them I want them within reach twenty-four hours a day. Got that?'

'Sure, Sid.'

'Good. I'm going to bed. And you can piss off home as Nathan's staying over for a couple of days to keep an eye on things. You've got a holiday for forty-eight hours.'

'Thanks. I could do with a change of clothes.'

'You could indeed, son.'

The thunder and lightning woke Vince up at a little after 9 a.m. He lay in bed for several minutes staring at the rain cascading down the window and then went into the kitchen and made a cup of instant coffee. He was just about to make some toast when he heard his mobile warble back in the bedroom. Vince wasn't sure whether he wanted to answer it but its insistent and prolonged ringing made the decision for him – whoever was calling most definitely wanted to speak to him.

'Hello?' said Vince as he lay back on the bed and hoped it wasn't any aggro.

It was Sid and it was prime-cut aggro: 'You seen the news yet?'

'What news?'

'On the TV. The news on the TV?'

'No. I just woke up. What's happened?'

'Switch it on. The balloon's gone up. Meet me at the boardroom at twelve. Got that?'

'Got it.'

The line went dead.

Ten minutes later Vince was looking at photographs of Phil and Leo on the television screen: black-and-white still photographs, mug-shot-like portraits, both of them staring out at you and looking like First Division psychos.

Definitely not flattering.

Where on earth did they get *those* from? thought Vince. Where on earth?

And now the woman announcer's voice: '...and identified by the police as Philip Waterhouse, used car dealer, and Leo Rimmer, a company director, both of East London.'

Then there was some footage of a bed-and-breakfast place somewhere in Margate with several police officers standing beside a plastic ribbon cordon thrown across the main entrance.

'...Also murdered were Mrs Peggy Hatchard, landlady of the Cozy Towers, and two of her guests whose identity the police are not releasing until next-of-kin have been traced.'

A uniformed cop appeared on screen next talking into camera. 'This is the most horrific crime ever in the Isle of Thanet's history...full investigation...every available officer... no stone unturned...members of the public...come forward...confidentiality....'

But Vince was no longer listening, he was in a state of disbelief at what he was hearing. None of this could be true, could it? Phil and Leo gone, dead? Rubbed out?

Executed? *And* a landlady *and* her guests?

What was going on down there in Margate?

Where was it leading?

Vince lit a cigarette without thinking and stared at the rain on the windows.

The only thing he could be sure of was, in fact, where it was leading.

That was the one certainty.

The only one.

Sid was sitting at the head of the boardroom table gazing into infinity, saying nothing and distractedly drawing on a cheroot. Vince was sitting on his left and Nathan on his right. The silence was oppressive.

Vince was thinking of Margate and putting himself in the position of whoever was behind the villainy down there. First there was Lionel – the genesis of this catalogue of murder, and there's not much we can say about him at this stage. Then we went down for the funeral. The funeral. Well, that was on the books. Anyone could have found out when the funeral was to take place and then put themselves about and kept an eye on the proceedings. That would explain Harry, the 'opportunistic' death.

But why didn't they try something bigger that time? Why just Harry?

Because…because there's just one of them? Is that the reason? Could be. Could not be. Could be any number of reasons. A lot of coulds.

Then there's Phil and Leo….

Now, nobody can keep tabs on who comes and goes to Margate. There's thousands of people, holidaymakers and day-trippers, motorists, delivery guys, and all the rest.

Phil and Leo must have signalled their presence there somehow, or, rather, word must have got through that they were there. Somebody knew they were there and what they were doing and that's when their cards were marked. Someone gave the word to someone – there are two guys here and they're looking into you-know-what.

That narrows it down a bit.

Narrows it down from the whole of the Isle of Thanet to just those people Phil and Leo had a chat with about…you-know-what.

That's a lot less people to deal with.

So, you just go down there, make some inquiries, and our mystery man or men will come looking for you. They'll be on your case right away. Just make sure you're ready, alert and prepared.

Vince's mind wandered back to those days out in Margate in the early 1970s, those summer days that seemed to last for ever, the beautiful young girls, the laughter and the excitement of youth, and all a quarter of a fucking century ago….

The door opened and a half-cut Wally slouched into the room waving a copy of *The Times*. 'Good day, Sidney, and good day to you too, gentlemen.'

There were a few murmurs and nods and Sid barked, 'Sit down, Wally, and tell me what you've found out and skip all the bullshit and colour.'

Wally pulled out a chair and eased himself into it. 'Is there any refreshment available, perchance?'

Sid pointed his cheroot at Wally and said, 'Start talking. What've you found out? What's going on down there then?'

'Early days, early days, Sid!'

'Get on with it, Wally, or you'll be instant landfill, and I mean that!'

'It seems, or so my little boy in blue at the seaside tells me, that they have two theories. Two theories, I might add, that are not mutually exclusive. One is that they were shot because of gangland drug dealings, the other is that it was to do with one little firm muscling in on another little firm's slot machines. Take your pick.'

'So,' says Sid, 'they've got it down as small time?'

'In the great scheme of things, *small* time, yes,' replied Wally. 'But we must hope that their inquiries into Phil and Leo don't lead them to your front door, Sid.'

'Fat chance, and even if they did, so what? What can they say to me? Fuck all, that's what.'

'Let's hope so,' added Wally.

Vince looked across at Wally and said, 'Were Phil and Leo killed by the same gun?'

'It appears so,' answered Wally. 'It was a .45 calibre bullet in both cases, but forensic still have to confirm they were fired from the same gun.'

Vince shot a glance at Sid – they both knew what the other was thinking: Lionel was killed with a .45 calibre slug too.

'And they reckon Phil was shot about an hour after Leo?' continued Vince.

'That's the thinking, but I don't think that's been scientifically proven yet,' stated Wally. 'And the landlady and her guests had .45s in them too. The police believe they chanced upon the gunman as he was leaving, so he let them have it too. They're not regarded as being connected in any way with the case.'

'And what I want to know,' coughs Sid, 'is how come they found Phil's body so soon in that abandoned place? And how did they connect him?'

Wally took a swig of something from his hip flask, wiped his mouth on his jacket sleeve, sighed, and said, 'Some kids were playing there, but the Old Bill were already aware of him from the register at the little hotel place. That simple, old boy. When they found him they knew who he was. Also, he had a book of matches on him with the hotel's name printed on it.'

Vince wanted to know if the coppers had any leads?

Wally smiled. 'If they have, the two top dogs are keeping it to themselves, but from what my boy on the ground says, they haven't even got a fart in a jar. They've got nothing. There's probably sixty officers out in the field now turning over every little toe-rag in the area, hoping they're going to beat some information out of someone. There's a lot of pressure on them to come up with the goods, and they'll be cutting corners like a bespoke tailor.'

'They made a connection with my brother yet?' Sid demanded.

'I shouldn't have thought so. How could they?' murmured Wally. 'Even if they did, where's that going to get them? That's a dead end.'

Sid winced at the reminder and resented Wally for stating the fact. It was also the matter-of-fact no-question-about-it way that this arsehole from Fleet Street said it.

Yeah, it may be a dead end right now, but it's not going to stay a dead end, I'll see to that all right. You can bet on that, thought Sid.

That evening at the club, in the back office, Sid was spread out on the sofa with nothing on but his boxer shorts being given a foot massage by a young blonde cutie who worked as a hostess out front. His eyes were closed and he was silent save for the occasional murmur of relaxation.

Vince was sitting at the desk in a pool of light from an

Anglepoise examining a street map of Margate and the Isle of Thanet. He hadn't been able to find one in London so he'd phoned a bookshop down in Ramsgate and with his VISA card got them to post him one.

Maps had always fascinated Vince, ever since he was a child and he'd discovered the one-inch Ordnance Survey sheets. They were invitations to mystery, romance and history, but the purpose now was a little more tangible.

Here's Margate station, here's Dreamland, Marine Terrace, Cecil Square, the ancient part of town here around the Market Square, the old High Street. Here's the coast, Nayland Rock, the harbour, the promenade, here are groynes and slipways and rocks right around to Cliftonville.

And here are dozens and dozens of streets, getting bigger and bigger and longer and longer the further they are from the original nucleus of the small fishing village that was Margate's beginning.

Somewhere down there, thought Vince, in one of these streets is a living, breathing human being who has the answers. He gets up in the morning, eats and drinks, sleeps, watches television, goes shopping, gets laid, and has the key to the mystery. Somewhere there. He could live there in Madeira Road or there in Railway Terrace, or possibly there in Love Lane, or even Zion Place?

But he's there somewhere.

And he's waiting.

He.

Vince was more convinced than ever now that they were dealing with *him*, one person. Perhaps one or two more. A gang or group wouldn't sit on their arses down there waiting. No. They'd be up here, taking the initiative, getting active. Searching us out.

Him.

He.

Yeah, perhaps one or two helpers, that's all.

He was sitting down there, patient and cunning, biding

his time, waiting for us to go down there, waiting for us to enter his web.

Luring us down there.

He's a cool and collected customer, somebody who's not going to rush it, he's got all the time in the world.

And he wants to do it on his patch.

He's slowly chip, chip, chipping away at Sid's strength. He's incrementally getting through to the guv....

Vince had noticed this particularly in the last fortnight or so. Sid was getting nervy, his mind would wander, he'd make mistakes, overlook things. Not like the Sid of old. True, he's putting a brave and hearty face on it all, but he isn't the guy he used to be. His mind is dwelling on things, wandering off. Sid's aware of this too because he's compensating all the time, starting just too many new ventures and schemes, moving on to another one before the first is completed.

Vince had noticed a thousand little changes in his behaviour.

'He's fallen asleep,' said a chirpy female voice in the broad vowels of South Londonese.

Vince looked up from the map, refocused his eyes, and saw the 'bunny' girl standing at the foot of the sofa, her hands moving down over her hips as she straightened her bodice.

'He's gone off,' she added.

Vince said, 'He's had a long day. Thanks.'

'Your feet don't need no attention then?'

'Not just this minute,' replied Vince, smiling at the girl.

She returned his smile and left the room quietly.

Vince returned to the map, his eyes wandering over and searching the roads and streets of Margate as if an answer were to be found here in front of him.

It was the early hours of the morning and the streets were empty. Vince was chauffeuring Sid home in the Jaguar.

Vince glanced at Sid in the front passenger seat. Sid had

been silent since they left the club. He'd just sat there staring ahead and saying nothing. There was an aura about him that Vince found disturbing.

The silence was broken by Sid as they passed under the Archway bridge. 'I can't get my mind off this. It's getting to be obsessive.'

Vince knew what he meant, but wasn't sure how to reply, not that Sid wanted any reply as he almost immediately continued with, 'I'm only going to rest when all this is resolved and we have the answers. Not until then. Not before.'

'There's not a lot we can do right now,' volunteered Vince.

'I know,' said Sid. 'We've got to be patient and just sit it out. There's no use us going down Margate with the Old Bill swarming all over the place. We'd soon get sucked up into the investigation. We've got to wait and see what they come up with.'

'Right, Sid.'

'Anyway, summer's upon us. We've got the new casino to open in Swansea and we got the annual Las Vegas trip to keep us busy. That'll keep our minds off it, won't it, eh? Give us plenty to think about?'

Sid followed this with a hollow laugh which Vince echoed.

'Yeah,' said Sid, 'we're not going to let this get on top of us, are we?'

'No, Sid, we're not.'

4: Colour Me Gone

SID AND VINCE RETURNED from Las Vegas at the end of September. The trip had been part holiday and part business. Sid had developed some new contacts and 'opportunities' in the fields of slot machines and gaming and he was eager and anxious to get these 'opportunities' developing. But eagerness and anxiety were not enough, as Vince knew too well. Such projects also required care and attention to detail and planning at every level. Sid wouldn't cough to the fact that the events in Margate were eating away at him, but then he didn't need to as Vince noticed it easily enough.

Nathan picked them up at Heathrow and the first thing Sid did was get on the blower to Gershon at the club and tell him that he wanted Wally and Lucksford for lunch tomorrow at the Ivy, 1 p.m. sharp, and *no* excuses.

We're back on the treadmill, thought Vince.

The investigation of Phil and Leo's deaths, and not forgetting those of the landlady and her guests, a crime now dubbed the 'Margate Massacre' by the tabloids, had been slowly wound down as leads and clues (and even a motive) failed to emerge. It started with well over fifty officers on the case in April and now, a little over five months later, there were just six uniformed officers left on the case sorting and filing paperwork and never leaving the office.

The one positive result of the investigation was that the Isle of Thanet was currently the most crime-free zone in the whole of Albion. The investigating officers, zealous to a man, had turned over everyone they could think of and as a result many unknown and undreamt of villainies came to light that resulted in a goodly number of local cons getting free board and lodging at Her Majesty's expense for varying lengths of time. And those cons that weren't rumbled knew the only thing they could do, pro tem, was keep their heads down and go about their lawful business. They wouldn't dare chance anything else.

The 'Margate Massacre' had been shunted off the front pages and, indeed, even the inside pages by the 'Harpenden Horror', an excursion in carnage that took place in a small town in Hertfordshire: a local Tory councillor ran amok with his shotgun and killed seven shoppers in the High Street and wounded dozens more before being taken out by a police marksman.

At least, people said, there was a reason for Margate, even if they didn't know what that reason was, but Harpenden? What reason was there for *that*? It couldn't have been because this geek had been asked to leave the town golf club, could it?

Sid and Vince's hopes of the Margate 'thing' being solved had been raised and then dashed on two occasions since April. The first was in May when a bloke named Willy Nudds had walked into the police station down there and confessed to being responsible for the shootings. The police got a bit too excited and made an announcement that they believed they had the killer, but on the following day it was revealed that Nudds had been an inmate in a locked ward at some Victorian mental hospital near Dartford when the crimes were committed.

Then, in August, the police got a phone call from a deserted wife who said her husband was the murderer. The police raided an address in nearby Herne Bay and found an unlicensed .45 calibre Colt secreted away behind the washing-machine and promptly arrested chummy that evening when he arrived home from repairing photocopiers. All very well and good, except that the bullets from this .45 calibre didn't match those found in and about the deceased in the massacre. Chummy was done for illegal possession and claimed in mitigation that he only had the pistol for self-protection in the event of 'West Indians, Indians and Jews' rising up to overthrow the Aryan races as was detailed in *The Protocols of the Illuminati*, a book he had been given by a mate at work who knew a thing or two about what was really going on in the world.

Sic transit, but not *gloria*.

Vince was lying on his bed smoking a joint and listening to a Charlie Parker CD. He was inhaling deeply and holding it down as long as he could, then very slowly exhaling. It felt wonderful to be back in his own place doing nothing. Doing absolutely fucking nothing. Just having a joint and going with the music, that's all.

Now the joint had gone out and nothing Vince did could coax it back to life. He turned over and reached across to the bedside table for his lighter and as he did so he was immediately confronted with two faces, two framed faces: Lisa, his girlfriend or, rather, ex-girlfriend, who he hadn't seen since April, and Dominic his son, a colour snap taken some ten years ago when he was only five. Vince couldn't bear to remember when it was he last saw Dom, that would be too painful, but he consoled himself with the fact that Patty, his ex-wife, was a good mother and looked after him. He'd grow up to be a fine boy. Indeed he was a fine boy.

A couple of tears appeared in the corners of Vince's eyes.

He picked up the telephone and dialled Lisa's number. It rang a few times and then the answering machine kicked in with Lisa's voice: *Hi, this is Lisa. I'm sorry I can't take your call right now, but please leave your name and number after the music.* There were several electronic bleeps and then a few bars of a waltz that sounded like it was coming from a music-box and then a loud bleep and then…silence.

Vince didn't know what to say. He wanted to say something, but he couldn't. He looked into the receiver as if this could suggest something, but nothing came. He hung up, rolled another joint and took a few more hits.

He picked the phone up again and dialled another number. A man's voice answered with a hello?

'Tim? It's Vince.'

'Vince. How are you? Susan and I were only talking about you this morning. How amazing!'

'I'm glad you haven't forgotten me. And how's business?'

'Pretty good. The restaurant's doing fantastically well and people are coming from all over Norfolk, and even London, to visit us.'

'And the hotel?' asked Vince.

'Pretty damn good, if you must know.'

Vince took another hit and said, 'Are you still looking for a partner to buy in?'

'If his name's Vince we are.'

'Good. I want in. I've had enough of it down here. It's time I moved on.'

'What's Sid going to say? How's he going to survive without you?'

'That's his problem. I haven't said anything yet, but I will. I will after I've got one little job out the way. I want to be up by the end of the year.'

'That's great. I'll get the solicitors drawing up a contract. We can have you installed in a little cottage with roses growing up it by the New Year.'

'I couldn't think of anything better,' replied Vince.

'Listen, come up soon for a weekend or something. We've got a new boat in the harbour and we're out most weekends fishing and carousing. You'll have a good time.'

'I will. It sounds good.'

'Great.'

'Give my love to Susan and the family. I'll call you in the week.'

'Do that.'

Vince lay back on the bed and took a few more hits as the opening bars of the *52nd Street Theme* jumped out from the four speakers....

Yeah, a quiet life in Wells-next-the-Sea...a cottage with roses...some sea fishing...a bit of dope now and then...a *rapprochement* with Patty...perhaps she and Dom could even come up at weekends? The good life, yeah.

What more could you want, eh?

What more?

The Ivy restaurant mid-afternoon on a Thursday. Half empty. Islands of diners at different tables. Half-heard whispers and murmurings punctuated with laughter that decays as soon as it begins.

In a corner table there's Sid and Vince with Wally and Lucksford from Scotland Yard. Wally's helping himself to his fourth glass of wine, oblivious to the white sauce that is slithering down his waistcoat. Vince's mind is partially elsewhere, dreaming of Wells-next-the-Sea and the quiet, hassle-free life that awaits him up there on the Norfolk coast. Sid is narrowly focused, he's thinking Margate, Margate *and* Margate. He's obsessed with the events and they haunt every waking minute of his life and most of the unwaking ones too, but he's like a psycho and knows how to cover it up and project a patina of normality. Nobody'll suspect, nobody'll get through to him. He's on a terminal course is our Sid.

Lucksford picks at his fish like a cat who has reservations about what was just put in his bowl and says, in a slow and considered manner, 'It's like this, Sidney. Their investigation produced nothing. No-thing. They didn't even come up with a used condom.'

'So what are they doing now?' demanded Sid.

'What can they do? The case is still open, but they've exhausted all leads and hunches. There's nothing more they can do...except...wait for something to turn up and if it doesn't, that's the end of it. You've seen this happen before. You know how these things go.'

'But this was my brother...*and* Harry and Phil and Leo!'

Lucksford dabbed the corners of his mouth with the napkin, looked above his spectacles towards Sid and said, 'Perhaps you should give the Chief Constable of Kent a call? He'd be an attentive listener, I'm sure.'

'Don't get sarky,' cautioned Sid.

'Until fresh evidence appears this is the end of the line,' added Lucksford.

Sid was incensed. 'All this money it costs us and the police just walk away from a series of murders?'

'Easy does it,' said Wally.

Lucksford would not be drawn. 'The police aren't God. And them walking away from crimes they can't crack has, Sidney, benefited you in the past...if memory serves.'

Sid ignored the pointed remark and turned to Wally. 'What you got then? What you come up with?'

Wally finished pouring himself a further glass of wine, smiled and said, 'Well, old bean, there's not a lot I can add to what the Chief-Superintendent has said. That's the state of play. I did hear a whisper though that the local bobbies thought there was a French connection.'

'A French connection?' said Sid, amazed. 'A *French* connection?'

Lucksford replied for Wally. 'Don't bother your head

about it, Sid. This French nonsense was put about down there by the lads informally – to explain why they hadn't collared anyone. You know, French drugs connection. The perpetrators all fleeing back to France. Just a bit of bullshit the papers went along with.'

'That so?' asked Sid grudgingly.

'I'm afraid it is,' responded Lucksford.

Sid just stared ahead unblinking. Vince knew what was going through his mind all right. Sid was becoming, indeed *had* become, consumed with revenge and each day he seemed to shift into a higher gear. It wasn't just revenge now, but self-esteem too. All those jack-the-lads out there just waiting to step into Sid's shoes. If they thought Sid had gone weak on this they'd think their day of inheritance had come just a little bit closer. It would increase the chances of a challenge and they could do without that, not that it would be anything more than small-time aggro.

Sid knew he had to move. He'd been biding his time too long now. But he still had to be patient. He had to do it *his* way, the right way.

'It seems then,' said Sid, carefully weighing each word, 'that we are at the end of the line?' He looked at Lucksford and at Wally. They both nodded.

'It seems also,' Sid continued, 'that all we can do now is put it all behind us and get on with our lives...until such time as something turns up...whenever that may be.'

Wally and Lucksford nodded in agreement.

'A toast then, gentlemen!' said Sid raising his glass. 'A toast – to the future...and whatever she may hold! Your good health!'

The four glasses met in the centre of the table.

Vince was toasting Wells-next-the-Sea and his future there, but he kept these thoughts to himself. He'll do the Margate nose-around and then tell Sid he's on his bike and out of here.

Colour me gone.

———————

After the lunch Sid stormed into the back office at the casino and threw his attaché case on the desk. It hit the top and smashed the Tiffany lamp, sent the Mont Blanc desk-top pen set flying and knocked a decanter of Scotch over that then started to spill its contents.

'Fucking Jesus Christ! I mean *fucking* Jesus Christ! None of those idiots could even find their own arsehole with a torch and mirror! Fuck me!' stormed Sid. 'Fucking Jesus!'

Vince was fascinated by the Scotch spreading out over the desk and waterfalling over the edge, seeping into the drawers, being mopped up by the Persian rug, seeking a level.

Indicating the desk to Sid, Vince said, 'We should get someone in for that.'

'Fuck that!' screeched Sid. 'We've got more important things to worry about in this firm! We've got our fucking survival to think about, that's what!'

Sid slumped down on the sofa and held his head in his hands. He started sobbing, quietly at first and then louder.

Vince wasn't sure what to do. 'Fancy a drink, Sid? Might make you feel better?'

'Fuck a drink. The only thing that'll make me feel better is some resolution. That's what I need. And I need it fast, before everything starts coming apart.'

'I know,' whispered Vince, lighting up a cigarette and easing himself into a facing armchair.

Sid stopped sobbing and took the handkerchief out of his breast pocket. He started dabbing his eyes. 'I just can't believe it. All these coppers running around mob-handed for six months and they come up with shit. Can you believe it? I can't. Six murders — '

'Seven,' interrupted Vince, 'if we include Harry.'

'OK, *seven*. And they've got nothing. And we've got nothing either. How do people get away with something like that, eh? Somebody's behind it all right. Do they just vanish off the face of the earth or what? Leave no traces?'

Vince shrugged.

'And people are talking about me now. All this goes on, they say, and old Sidney Blattner hasn't...*can't* do a damn thing about it. They interpret it as sign of weakness, they do. They'll figure the firm's up for grabs...and we can't have that, old son, can we?'

'No, we can't,' replied Vince, 'and we won't have it.' But the passion and commitment were missing from Vince's words. Had Sid been the old Sid, the Sid of six months ago, he would have detected the creeping hollowness in Vince's voice, but now his loop of introversion blinded him. His hands were full figuring out his own thoughts. Figuring out other people's thoughts was now an alien labour.

'Anyway, Vince. We'll see what happens. It's all blown over and the Old Bill down there have gone home to bed. Wally and Lucksford think we've gone to sleep on it. Nobody knows.'

'Keep it that way. Only you and me know I'm going down there, right?'

'Right. If anyone asks I'll say you've gone to see some relatives up north. There's no reason why they shouldn't believe me. Good. Loose talk costs lives, as they used to say.'

'No, Sid. *Careless* talk costs lives. Loose lips sink ships,' said Vince.

'Yeah. They used to say that during the war. Where'd you get it from? Out of a *book*?'

Vince nodded and noted the disapproving way Sid pronounced the word book.

'When you leaving?' asked Sid, getting back to the mainstream of the conversation.

'First thing tomorrow morning.'

'Uh-huh. Take care.'

'I will.'

'And stay in touch.'

'I'll have my mobile with me.'

'You got everything you need?'

'I think so. But I could do with a dollop of good luck.'

'That's the one thing the firm can't supply. Here you have to supply your own.'

'I'm hoping.'

Vince thought this wasn't the exact perfect moment to tell Sid he wanted out. He'd do that as soon as the Margate Problem (as they had come to refer to it) was out of the way if, indeed, it was ever got out of the way. *And* if he survived it....

5: Keep Your Margate Joys…

THE ALARM WOKE VINCE at 7 a.m. An hour later he was showered and dressed, packed and ready. He phoned for a taxi and then gave Larry over on the Caledonian Road a bell to tell him he was on the way.

In the back of the cab Vince checked through the small suitcase to see that he hadn't forgotten anything: several changes of clothes, toiletry items, a file he'd put together on the case, a Thanet street map, a couple of Ordnance Survey maps, a pocket-size Olympus tape recorder and mike (should he have to go anywhere wired-up), his Sony Walkman and a couple of modern jazz CDs, three cases of .22 Remington flat-nosed ammo, a couple of bundles of £50 notes, a miniature telescope, a Gerber Multi-Plier tool, some pens and some notebooks. All that was missing was the break that would allow him to crack the problem and scarper off to Wells-next-the-Sea. Scarper off up there, yeah.

In his jacket pockets were his mobile phone, address book and his Swiss Army knife. In his shoulder holster was a .22 Walther semi-auto with a full mag. Small calibre, yeah, but effective when used correctly.

All dressed up and ready to party, thought Vince. All dressed up.

The black cab pulled up outside Larry's Used Autos just off the Caledonian Road up from Copenhagen Street. Vince got out, paid the driver and walked through to the side door.

The eponymous Larry, a big guy in his early forties who looked like a Hell's Angel, greeted Vince, gave him a big hug and said, 'She's ready outside. Follow me.'

Vince nodded and obeyed the instructions.

Out back was a vehicle that fitted Vince's requirements exactly: a car that was powerful and yet at the same time didn't warrant a second look. What Larry had come up with was a black, unbadged VW VR6 that was five years old and could do with a new paint job. It was perfect. As Phil once said to Vince about some old saloon he was then driving – the only thing you could pull in that is a caravan.

'All checked and in fine shape,' said Larry. 'You'll fall in love with her.'

Wonderful, thought Vince.

'Just don't shunt it,' pleaded Larry.

'I won't,' replied Vince. 'I'll treasure her and she won't want to leave me.'

Vince pulled the VW's door shut as Larry wandered off to the local café for breakfast. Vince fancied a big greasy fry-up with, as Larry put it, 'all the trimmings including mush-rooms and black pudding,' but that would have delayed him. He wanted to get a move on. Get down to Margate, check out the town, get his bearings, get a feel for things.

Vince went to insert the key in the ignition and suddenly stopped. This was the real beginning of the Margate trip, he realised. It all starts now. Right now. Right here.

This is where it starts.

I'm on my own.

Do we all go through life taking bigger and greater chances until we finally overreach ourselves and meet our destiny?

Have I bitten off more than I can chew?

This was sobering.

Vince was committed to doing what he could to sort the Margate Problem. Christ, he'd lived with it long enough. Owed it to Sid. Yeah, do his bit down there and then with a clear conscience he'd turn around to Sid and say goodbye. Nothing Sid could object to then. He'd have to like it or lump it.

Get this sorted and then get out.

Up to Wells on the Norfolk coast.

Just got to get this sorted.

Vince pushed the key in and turned it. The big dependable engine started up, oozing confidence and horsepower.

The VW pulled out on to the Caledonian Road and headed south amidst the morning traffic.

It took a left on to the Pentonville Road and then continued straight on, past the Angel and down the City Road. The sun was now peering out from the clouds and it was beginning to feel like a spring day, even if it was the end of September.

Vince went down through the east of the City, turned down the Commercial Road and after innumerable delays was heading south into the Rotherhithe Tunnel and under the Thames.

Once out of the tunnel it was a pretty clear run down through Deptford and up to Blackheath as all the traffic was heading towards London, not away from it.

On the dual carriageway of the old Dover Road Vince gave the accelerator some welly and the VW shot forward, as Sid would say, like a bat out of hell. Vince was pushed back in the seat as a mighty roar propelled the car forward.

In no time it had gone from 50 to 100 m.p.h. Vince eased off the pedal and gave a quick glance to each of the mirrors just to make sure the traffic cops weren't about. The last thing he needed was the aggro of being pulled over and whatever that might lead to....

Vince slowed down to about 55 m.p.h. and kept to the nearside lane. He wanted to be anonymous and invisible on this trip, just part of the scenery and nothing else.

South-eastwards through those interminable suburbs of London and then into the open country and soon over the River Medway near Rochester, up the winding hill that hugs the chalk downs and then straight ahead.

Vince wasn't thinking of the Margate Problem, he was thinking of Tim and Susan and the hotel-restaurant up in Wells. He'd be there soon, once this immediate business was put out to graze. A hassle-free life. An aggro-free life. Getting up when he wanted to and going to bed whenever. Fishing at sea, tending the garden and just lazing about. He couldn't wait.

He pulled in at a motorway service station and got a coffee and chicken salad sandwich to go. Back in the car he looked at an OS map of the East Kent area, sipped the coffee, ate the sandwich and decided that as he was ahead of schedule he'd take not the direct route to Margate, but instead the picturesque detour via Canterbury and Sandwich arriving at his destination from the south.

There ahead were the towers of Canterbury cathedral dominating the small city and its environs, rising majestically into the haze of an early autumnal day. There, straight ahead, seemingly at the end of the motorway.

One of Vince's earliest memories was being led around the cathedral by his mother and father who had taken an afternoon off from hop-picking...hop-picking...the nearest they ever got to a holiday in his childhood. The traditional London inner-city working-class sojourn. But now? Well, there is no working class left any more (just an underclass, which is not the same thing) and, as for hops, whatever became of them? They largely seem to have disappeared from Kent, along with the orchards.

Vince followed the road down and around but his mind was trying to rescue the fading and dissolving memories of his earliest years, and when it occurred to him he should be taking a turning off somewhere it was already too late and he was a third of the way towards Dover. Fuck it, he thought. So he continued on through the rolling chalkland, glanced off Dover, and up through Deal and Sandwich, finally alighting upon the Isle of Thanet by the sweep of Pegwell Bay.

After a few wrong turnings somewhere at the back of Ramsgate Vince found the Margate Road and sped north along it, past hypermarkets, tired farmland, and nineteenth-century artisans' terraces rendered in pebble-dash and painted with colours taken from the palette of an early Technicolor film.

And then ahead on a prominence with the sea beyond was Margate.

Margate.

Sitting there waiting for him like some fat tart sourly saying, 'What kept you, *then*?'

This is it, thought Vince.

Margate.

Margate?

The name sounded like something you spread on bread. Funny that, thought Vince, it had never occurred to me. *Mar*-gate.

Vince parked up in the station forecourt and walked across to the seafront. The gulls were swooping around above him crying out for scraps to eat or whatever it is they cry out for. Those cries high in the air that told you this was the seaside.

The air was fresh and chill and the sea seemed even bluer than the blue sky. There were still little crowds of holidaymakers here and then and even some determined folks in swimming costumes. *They* were not going to be cheated of a dip in the sea (Vince remembered that the English Channel didn't begin until you got further east, to the North Foreland, so, strictly speaking, as this was not the North Sea it must actually be the estuarine Thames).

On Vince's right was Marine Terrace with its bingo halls and amusement arcades and novelty shops and then there was the stark 1930s brickwork of Dreamland's cinema rising high above the front and, looming over Dreamland, a 1960s tower block that seemed to rise to the very heavens, dwarfing everything else.

At the other end of Marine Terrace the ground rose quite sharply to the old part of town with the fading elegance of houses and terraces from the early 1800s now metamorphosed, at ground level, into more bingo halls and fast food dives, bars and lounges. *And* the restaurant where they were when Harry the Chauffeur disappeared.

There's a funny little clock-tower at the foot of the hill and a small park behind it and then, further to the left, the old harbour as the seafront curves around out of sight.

Vince flicked the filter tip of his finished Marlboro Light over the esplanade and into the sand.

There's a problem that's got to be sorted and the sooner it's sorted the sooner I'm up there in Wells.

It's showtime as they say.

Then the mobile rang.

'Hello?' said Vince.

It was Sid. 'What you up to, son?'

'Just got here. I'm taking the sea air.'

'Uh-huh. Thought I'd give you a quick bell to see everything's OK.'

'Yeah. Haven't been here long enough for anything good, bad or ugly to happen yet.'

'You keep in touch.'

'Yeah,' said Vince. And he closed the phone.

Now to find somewhere decent but low key to kip down. Some little, anonymous bed-and-breakfast place where they'd only notice you if you didn't pay up. There were hundreds of such places in Margate, so it shouldn't be too difficult. But Vince wanted somewhere with a loft and a back entrance.

That might prove a little more difficult.

Vince walked back to the car and then drove along the seafront to the area beyond the harbour where there was a proliferation of small private hotels wrought out of the early nineteenth-century villas that had originally been built for the fashionable classes who had come here to take the seawater.

Originally, but that was a long time ago....

Vince pulled into a turning and parked up. The area was busy with traffic and pedestrians and it seemed as safe a place to park as any. Grabbing his case he walked down to the front and started looking for a base.

The hoteliers of Margate always seemed to go in either for the prosaic or the exotic name. For every Elm Lodge Private Hotel there was a Buenos Aires Guest House, for every Fairbanks Hall Hotel there was a Luxor Luxury Hotel. Vince wondered what decided the owners to alight upon one over the other? What arcane formularies were at work here in the choice of a name?

Several of the hotels Vince tried had access from the back or the side but either there were no rooms available on the top floor ('They are our *private* quarters') or if there were they were bereft of a ceiling trapdoor.

Finally, Vince found the perfect place opposite the Winter Gardens. It was called the Trade Winds Hotel on Fort Crescent and it was spot on. You could walk down the side of one of the hotels it backed on to, nip across an alley and enter by the side, and the room (overlooking the sea, yet!) had an entrance in the centre of the ceiling for the attic. All this, and only £27 a night. Not bad at all.

Vince insisted on paying for five nights in advance and in cash despite the landlady saying it wasn't necessary. But Vince figured this would get her off his back until day six.

He went up to his room and had a snooze and thought to himself that this would be the first and last night he would sleep in the bed, because as from tomorrow he'd be announcing his presence in Margate and who knows who might be seeking him out.

That evening he went for a stroll along the seafront and down by the harbour. It was a warmish evening and there was a salty-tasting breeze in the air. The night sky was clear and the stars looked like iced crystals suspended in the heavens. There were knots of mostly young holidaymakers carousing about, the girls screaming and the guys' laughter cutting through the traffic. Vince had some fish and chips in a little café near Market Square and then wandered into the Bull's Head pub for a vodka and orange. He sat in the corner and looked through a list of names and addresses of contacts. Tomorrow the inquiry would begin. Tomorrow he'd start hauling ass, as they say.

As he finished the drink Vince looked across the pub at the faces gathered around the bar, all oblivious to him. They're all going about their business, young and old, knocking back their lagers and their gin and tonics and their shandys. Perhaps someone here has the answer? But if not here, somewhere in Margate there's someone who knows what it's all about.

It's just a case of finding them before they find me.

It's that simple thought Vince.

That simple.

And that difficult too.

But perhaps it was easier to let them find him?

Most people had left the Trade Winds' Breakfast Room when Vince walked in. He took a corner seat by a table that overlooked the garden at the rear of the hotel. A young blonde, scarcely out of her teens, showed him a menu and he ordered a traditional fry-up with a pot of coffee.

The girl was back with the coffee before Vince had even had a chance to scan the front page of the *Daily Mail*. He thanked her and asked her what her name was.

'Cheryl,' she said.

'Uh-huh. Is this your mum and dad's place?'

'Nuh. I just work here.'

'You grow up here?'

'Yeah. I was born in Cliftonville.'

'Good,' said Vince. 'So you know your way about?'

'Think so.'

'Know a good shop that sells camping gear?'

'Camping gear?'

'You know, tents and stuff.'

'Tents, yeah. Thanet Outdoors. Up the top of the High Street, just past Cecil Square,' replied Cheryl.

'Thanks,' said Vince as he returned to the newspaper.

It was always Vince's policy to cultivate contacts. You never know when you might need them. Little Cheryl here might not know her way about the local council or the underworld, but she knows the area, knows other people.

Vince took out the contacts list and ran his finger down the names. He stopped at the copper's, his home number. He dialled it up on the mobile and it rang. An answering machine then cut in. Vince terminated the call and dialled Mrs Spooner. She answered, an elderly genteel and rather tremulous voice.

'Mrs Spooner?'

'Yes?'

'I'm a close friend of Sid Blattner's. He wanted me to come around and see you.'

'Oh, Sidney. How is he?'

'He's fine. Sends his regards. Are you at home this morning?'

'Yes. I do my shopping on Wednesdays.'

'OK if I pop around, then?'

'Yes, of course. Do you have my address?'

'I do. Say in about an hour or so?'

'I'll put the kettle on.'

'Thanks.'

As Vince closed the phone Cheryl arrived with a large plate upon which were fried eggs, fried bread, tomatoes, mushrooms, bacon, black pudding and something Vince couldn't identify but which, nonetheless, looked tasty enough.

'We got seconds if you want,' offered Cheryl.

'I think this'll do me.'

'Yeah. Well, just shout. OK?'

'Got you.'

Vince wolfed his way through the breakfast and barely left anything, finished the coffee, thanked Cheryl and was off walking down the road in less than twenty minutes.

It was a bright chill day again and the seafront was empty except for groups of gulls picking over yesterday's refuse and the remains of last night's take-aways. There was little traffic.

Vince got to the old High Street and took out the street map of Margate to check he was going in the right direction. He cut across a couple of roads and was soon in Victoria Road where Mrs Spooner lived.

She lived in a ground floor flat in a late-Victorian house that had seen better days. The brickwork was in need of repointing, paint was peeling from the window frames, hardboard had replaced the glazing in several windows on the first floor, and there was an insinuating smell of damp.

Mrs Spooner was a small woman in her sixties with grey hair. She was well dressed and her manner and speech were 'respectable' working class. She invited Vince in to a spotlessly clean flat that almost creaked under the weight of statuettes and knick-knacks that seemed to occupy every available horizontal space. She bade Vince sit down on the sofa while she went out to the kitchen to prepare the tea.

Vince gazed around the room and looked at the dozens of framed photographs, presumably her children and their children, and also some old black-and-white photographs of weddings and people long dead. The past sat heavily in this flat.

Mrs Spooner returned with a tray bearing two bone china cups and saucers, a pot of tea, and a plate of custard creams that she placed on the coffee table. Vince thanked her. She sat opposite him and poured the tea while explaining she had lost her husband a year ago to the day. Vince said he was sorry to hear that. She replied, matter of factly, that we all have to go when we have to go.

'What about Lionel then?'

Mrs Spooner stopped sipping her tea and thought for a moment before answering. 'I think there is a difference between going when God says your time is up, like dear Ernest did, and being...you know...done *away* with, like Lionel.'

'That's true,' said Vince, now on his third biscuit. 'Do you have any theories as to why he was done away with?'

'Not a day has gone by since it happened that I haven't thought...*why*?'

'Any ideas?'

'There must be a reason, but I don't know what it is. Perhaps they mistook him for someone else? That's all I could think of...they just mistook him.'

'How long did you know Lionel?'

'I knew his mother first. Met her in the early 1950s just about the time I was getting married. Knew him soon after that. And then when his mother was getting on a bit I went to work in the shop. Part time, first of all, just to help out. Then it got full time and that must have been about 1965...perhaps a little later.'

'So you knew him pretty well for the last forty years or so.'

'Pretty well,' said Mrs Spooner as she placed her cup and saucer back on the tray.

'Tell me something about him.'

'Like what?'

'Like...who were his friends? What did he like doing? What sort of bloke was he? Did he have any peculiarities?'

'He didn't have any peculiarities I don't think. He was

very *ordinary*, you know.'

'What about his friends?'

'Didn't really have any of those either. He used to go to the bowling club regularly. They knew him there but they weren't what you call *friends*. None of them ever came back to the flat – you know, the flat above the shop. So you wouldn't really call them friends. Not friends.'

'Who was close to him?'

'His brother?'

'But he didn't see much of Sid, did he?'

'Suppose not.'

'Who was close to him?'

'There wasn't anyone I can think of.'

'Who was closer to him than you?'

'I don't think there was anyone. Not that I can think of.'

'So you were the one closest to him then?'

'I wouldn't say I was close. It's just that I worked there full time so I saw a lot of him. Lionel wasn't someone you got close to. Least I didn't. He liked to keep himself to himself.'

Vince was building up a picture of Lionel being a total social zeroid. A guy who had no friends, never went anywhere, didn't do anything hardly…except….

'So, Mrs Spooner, you're saying he just ran the newsagent's, went bowling sometimes and that was it? There was nothing else?'

'More tea, dear?' she asked.

Vince nodded and Mrs Spooner poured another cup while she spoke. 'They've all been asking me these questions. I saw the police several times and they were very nice. They didn't seem to believe me at first, but there was nothing I could tell them.'

'Did he ever go on holiday?'

'No.'

'Did he go to church?'

'You mean the synagogue?'

'Yes.'

'No.'

'Never had any girlfriends?'

'No.'

'Was never married?'

'No.'

'Any hobbies?'

'Bowling, if you call that a hobby. But I doubt if you'll find much out from the bowling club. They're all too old and past it up there. Hardly know what day of the week it is they don't.'

'Did he have any dreams, plans, ambitions? Anything like that?'

'He always said he'd like to buy a nice house up in Cliftonville somewhere and retire there.'

'Uh-huh. He had the money. Why didn't he do that?'

'Don't know. Too busy running the shop.'

Vince was running out of questions.

It wasn't that Mrs Spooner wouldn't have noticed any-thing – she was bright and alert – it was just that there was nothing to be noticed. The guy got up in the morning, ran his newsagent business and then went to bed. Sometimes he would go bowling and that was about it...aside from, that is, the visits to the massage parlour, but better not say anything about them right now.

'Tell me about the night it happened, Mrs Spooner.'

'Which night?'

'The night he was done away with. The last time you saw him.'

'Oh, *that* night. It was just like any other night. I left about 6.30 p.m. and he was out back doing the books. I said goodnight and he said goodnight and I came home.'

'He didn't seem in any way different that night, or that afternoon...or the days preceding?'

'No. The same as ever. Cheerful, getting on with the business. Nothing special.'

'So, you left about 6.30 p.m. and the next thing you know is a phone call from the Old Bill.'

'The Old Bill?' inquired Mrs Spooner.

'Sorry, the police.'

'Oh, yes. The Old Bill. The police.'

'Uh-huh. That was the next thing you knew?'

'Yes it was. I had to go down and identify him.'

'Do you know anything about what happened to him after you left?'

'No. The police said they thought he might have gone for a walk because there were no signs of anything, you know, like a struggle at the shop or in the flat. Once he locked up at night that was it. He wouldn't open up again unless he knew you.'

'Did he go for walks?'

'If he went out it was usually to get something, to do a bit of shopping. He didn't go out for *walks*.'

Vince finished the cup of tea and polished off the seventh and final custard cream. What more could he ask her? Could there be something she knows that she doesn't appreciate the significance of? Something locked away in her mind that could cast a bit of light on the mystery?

If there was something he didn't have the time to sit there patiently for half of eternity firing scatter-gun questions. Those monkeys on the typewriters would come up with the complete works of Shakespeare before he'd get what he wanted.

She might just know something, some little thing, but Vince didn't have the time.

He took out his notebook and wrote down his name and mobile number and tore the page out and gave it to Mrs Spooner. 'I'm staying at the Trade Winds hotel on Fort Crescent. If you think of anything give me a call. Or if there's anyone else that could help, get them to call.'

'Of course, dear. Of course.'

Vince walked back the way he had come and then up past the hotel to the bowling club that was situated on the Eastern Esplanade at Cliftonville. There were a couple of games in progress and none of the participants looked much under the age of seventy.

Several signs said members only but as nobody stopped him Vince continued through the grounds to the refreshment pavilion. A couple of old geezers and dears, all dressed in white, sat in a group by the window. Vince went over to the bar and caught the attention of the barman who was down one end polishing glasses.

'You're a member, sir?' said the barman.

'No, but I'm with someone who is. They'll be joining me in a minute.'

'What'll you have?'

'Vodka and orange?'

'Certainly.'

As the guy prepared the drink Vince thought it probably unwise to engage him in any Lionel-related conversation. He'd keep to the members.

Vince took the drink outside and looked around to see if there were any likely candidates for interviewing. There were two old guys, both smoking pipes, at the top end of one of the greens.

Vince approached them.

'Fine day, today, eh?' said Vince in his best Home Counties accent.

'Spot of rain later this afternoon they say,' said the more portly of the two.

'What a pity,' Vince replied.

'Plants could do with it though,' the slimmer one said.

'Dare say they could,' replied Vince. 'I'm sorry, let me introduce myself. I'm Vincent Narraway.'

'Pleased to meet you. I'm Walter Camden and this is Harold Shipley,' said the fatter guy, extending his hand.

After the formalities were over Vince said he was down for the day tying up some loose ends in a life insurance settlement, one that related to a member of their club.

'And who would that be?' asked Shipley.

'Lionel Blattner,' replied Vince nonchalantly.

'Oh, Lionel! Old Lionel,' piped Camden.

'You knew him?' Vince inquired.

'Didn't really *know* him. He used to play up here regularly, but I can't say I knew him. Just played the odd game with him. He never did any of the *après*-bowling socialising, which is what most people join the club for. He didn't go in for any of that, did he, Harold?'

Harold sucked on his pipe, thought for a moment, scratched his nose, stifled a yawn and said, '*None* of that. No. Pity about what happened to him.'

'Ah-huh. Did anyone up here know him?' asked Vince, knowing full well what the answer would be.

Camden and Shipley looked at each other and shook their heads from side to side.

And that was that. Aside from Vince giving them his mobile and the name of where he was staying on the off-chance they or someone they knew had some titbit to pass on.

But that really was it.

Vince sensed that there was nothing to be garnered from the all-in-white crowd. The answers to the enigma surrounding Lionel's premature demise were not to be found on the smooth grass of the bowling club green.

He looked at the list of other bowling club members Phil had diligently put together: their names, addresses and phone numbers. Phil had come up with zilch and if he couldn't uncover anything Vince felt he'd be wasting his time going over the same ground. He'd pass on this lot for the time being.

So what does that leave?

Immediately, that is, an empty stomach.

Vince walked back along the front and past the clock-tower to the restaurant on the hill where he'd had lunch with Sid and Leo the day Harry disappeared.

The place was almost empty. Vince took a window seat and gazed across the sea. The waitress said she'd recommend the goulash, a speciality of the house, and Vince said that was fine with him. He looked around and didn't recognise anyone from his last visit, and nobody seemed to recognise him. So that was cool.

Vince dialled the copper's number again and a woman answered: 'Yes?'

The *Yes?* was said in a bored South London voice. This sounded like the wife all right.

Politeness and social foreplay would be wasted on this one, thought Vince. 'Terry about then?'

'Won't be in till about seven,' she replied managing to combine irritation, impatience and defiance in the same breath.

'OK, I'll call him then.'

She hung up.

Didn't even bother to ask who I was or if there was a message, thought Vince. I'll call old Terry tonight, see what he's got to say for himself.

The goulash was very passable and Vince left a couple of quid for the waitress who, he guessed correctly, was Hungarian.

Vince walked up the hill and along the High Street until he came to the camping shop Cheryl had told him about – Thanet Outdoors. There was a good selection of sleeping bags and Vince bought an expensive one, filled with Hollo-fil and a cheap one filled with nylon and also a kip mat for added comfort. And, lastly, a medium-sized Mag-Lite torch that caught his eye on the way out.

The young guy in the shop had directed him to a hardware shop further up the High Street where Vince bought an ultra-lightweight telescopic alloy ladder that extended to ten feet yet could be collapsed and carried under your arm. Just the job, thought Vince. Just the fucking job.

Carrying a large plastic bag with these newly acquired goods Vince headed back along the High Street and then down New Street to Lionel's shop. There it was in front of him, all boarded up now, BLATTNER'S NEWSAGENTS. A small shop by any standards and one that Vince guessed didn't have much passing holidaymaker trade even at the height of the summer season. No, this little corner shop just served the locality, the 'hood.

The sign above the shop looked like it had been there since the early 1960s. The different coloured paints had had the pigment burnt out of them by the sun and in many places the paint had peeled away completely leaving the wood exposed.

The only fresh looking thing about the place was the security boarding Sid had organised to prevent local tea-leaves and vandals from helping themselves (though to what? Vince wondered).

There were two floors above the shop and one of these was in the roof space. Vince guessed it was originally a cottage built in the 1700s with Victorian additions.

This was a little street that Margate the seaside resort had somehow passed by. There was nothing to attract the holidaymakers here and it didn't even appear to be on the way to anywhere. Just a quiet little backwater. The show was elsewhere.

Vince fumbled around in his pockets for the keys Sid had given him and then let himself in by the side door. There was a smell of damp and mustiness, air that had remained trapped here since Lionel had met his maker.

Ahead were the steep stairs leading to the flat above and to the right was a door leading into the shop.

Might as well have a sniff around the shop first, thought Vince. He tried several keys until he found the right one. The door was unlocked but it refused to open and it wasn't until Vince gave it his shoulder that it swung back.

Still-life at the newsagent's thought Vince as he glanced about the place. The shelves and the counters had been emptied of sweets and cigarettes by Mrs Spooner on Sid's instructions and all that was left now were the dated wooden fittings. There were fading newspapers on the counter and magazines in the racks and cans and bottles of drink here and there. An old manual cash register was open and empty by the far wall. Close to the street door were a few children's buckets and spades. Vince picked one of the spades up: it had a wooden handle. It must have been here for twenty years or more. When did they last use wood? They're all plastic now.

Vince went through to the office at the back: an old desk, a couple of worn leather chairs, a filing cabinet that looked pre-war, and a big black telephone with a dial and cloth-covered flex yet! There were posters of Margate on the wall and several calendars and also a list of Customers Who Are Not To Be Extended Credit. Could that be worth a second look? No. Not unless the refusal of a pack of twenty fags until Friday is considered sufficient reason in Thanet for a .45 through the cortex.

Vince sat down behind the desk, pulled open a couple of drawers and riffled through the papers – invoices from wholesalers, receipts, pens and pencils, raffle tickets, a newspaper delivery ledger, accounts and so on. Nothing else. Nothing of interest.

What was he hoping to find anyway? The place had been gone over several times by the police and by Phil and Leo and nobody had come up with a brass farthing. The chances of something significant still knocking about were zero.

Vince got up and went to the back door. He slid open the two bolts and turned the heavy lock. The door opened on to a small yard that was delimited by an old flint wall about six feet high. There were bundles of yellowing news-papers tied with string, a couple of metal rubbish bins, a bag of cement that had solidified, and a washing machine. The door on the far wall, secured with a sliding bolt, opened on to an alleyway wide enough for one car.

There was nothing to be seen up and down the alley except rubbish bins.

It occurred to Vince that someone could have easily gained access to the back of the shop, perhaps when Lionel was sitting in the office doing his paperwork, and got him out this way. Bundle him into a waiting car and that's that. Easy. Bob's your uncle. But there was no sign of a forced entry anywhere. How would they have got in?

Vince walked back in, carefully shutting the doors behind him. He looked around the office again and the shop in the hope that something of importance would leap out at him, but there was nothing.

Upstairs, I guess.

On the first floor was a sitting room, a kitchen, and a bathroom and lavatory. If you were shooting a film set in the 1950s or, indeed, the 1940s you could move in here and just start the camera rolling. Time had stood still up here, thought Vince. Nothing had changed in years.

The curtains were old and threadbare, the bulbous leather three-piece suite was worn, the carpet frayed. In one corner was a big radiogram and in another a polished wooden sideboard full of unopened bottles of spirits. The wallpaper had that sort of Paisley pattern on it Vince remembered from his childhood, and it was dull and stained and cloaked in cigarette smoke. Where the carpet ended actual linoleum began. Yes, the real McCoy. Your real, old linoleum, heavy and hard and unforgiving in a dark shit-like brown.

The mantelpiece was crammed with Toby jugs and gift goblets and in the centre, beneath a painting of some aged rabbi from *mittel* Europe, was one of those seven-pronged candlesticks you always see in Jewish homes.

There was a name for it, but Vince couldn't remember what it was.

There was also a heavy unpleasant smell to the place, as though a cat or something had crawled behind the curtains and died and was now decomposing.

The bathroom had a metal bath on legs, a massive hand-basin, and only an Ascot heater for hot water. The dark greenish paint on the walls was peeling. There were patches of damp on the exterior wall.

As for the lavatory, Vince had seen better appointed ones in Port Said back in his army days. A heavy cast-iron tank was set high in a corner, almost touching the ceiling, with a bare metal pipe coming down to the pan that was stained and surface-cracked beyond redemption.

The kitchen overlooked the back yard and that was quite the most pleasant thing about it. The gas stove stood on legs and deserved to be in a museum. A solid dining-room table took up most of the available space. Good old Lionel didn't give many swingin' dinner parties here.

Stairs not much wider than Vince's shoulders curved around to the next floor up, where there were two bedrooms. The front bedroom with a double bed was obviously Ma Blattner's. There was a veneer dressing table with an oval mirror, a bulky wardrobe (1940s utility), the massive double bed that almost came up to Vince's waist, a tallboy, an ottoman and net curtains on the window that were stained yellow with age. The velvet curtains hadn't been closed for years and when Vince attempted to close one of them the material came away in his hands. The windowsill was covered with dozens of dead wasps and ladybirds who had spent their last days clambering against the glass trying to reach the world beyond.

On the walls were some framed engravings of the old country and framed photographs of Blattner forebears who probably even Sid would have difficulty recognising.

The room hadn't changed much since Sid's mother had died, Vince guessed. Lionel had no reason to go in there and do anything, so he'd left it. This frozen frame of time.

Lionel's bedroom was tatty but at least it looked lived in. The curtains appeared twenty years old rather than forty and his bed seemed as though he'd bought it in the last ten years. There was a wardrobe, a writing bureau, and a bedside table upon which was a lamp and some books written in Hebrew.

Duvets hadn't entered Lionel's life. Above the sheets on the bed were several layers of blankets and a bulky eiderdown covered in a dark purple patterned material that resembled silk.

So this was where Lionel kipped down each night?

Vince sat down on the bed and lit a cigarette and gazed about the room and wondered why Lionel, who wasn't short of a bob or two, lived like this? It obviously suited him. His horizons were limited to the shop. He lived simply and his waking hours were centred on the shop. And that was it. He tended his business and went to sleep. There was nothing else...well, almost nothing else.

No, the reason for the execution wasn't to be found in Lionel's life, it was to be found in Sid's. No ifs, ands or buts.

Sid was where it began and Sid was where it would end. We've all been investigating the wrong individual. It's what Vince thought in the beginning and he knows it's true whether he's going to be around to discover it or not.

Vince wandered through the rooms again on the off-chance there might be some little clue he'd spot, but there wasn't. There's nothing here.

Nothing.

After grabbing his bag and locking up, Vince stood outside and gazed up and down the street. On one side of the shop was a run-down cottage that still had a couple of bottles of milk on the doorstep this late in the day and on the other side was a small junk shop aspiring to be an antique shop. The rest of the street was a mish-mash of gentrified cottages, church halls, and derelict sites ready for redevelopment.

A tranquil back street with scarcely any traffic and with the sounds of gulls rising above the distant humming from the seafront.

There was no reply from the cottage with the milk bottles so Vince decided to give the junk shop a whirl.

A bell on a spring rang as Vince pushed the door open.

The place was full of the sort of domestic detritus that arises from house clearances, but here and there were items of more than passing interest – a couple of fine magic lanterns, butterfly and insect cases, marble figurines and so on.

A man with a stoop and a bald head and a big grey moustache approached Vince. He wore pin-stripe trousers that were stained and covered in dust and an old pullover, again stained, over a grubby white shirt and a regimental tie.

'Is there anything you are particularly interested in? Anything I can show you?' The voice was educated and the pronunciation clipped and precise and it belied the man's shabby appearance.

'No. My name is Vince Narraway. I'm a family friend of the Blattners.'

'Oh, yes. Mr Blattner.'

'His brother asked me to pop down and check the shop.'

'I see. Yes. We'll miss not having him here. *So* convenient.'

'Did you know Lionel at all?'

'Just to say hello to. Not much more.'

'It's a big mystery to his family...what happened.'

'And to the rest of Margate as well, Mr Narraway.'

There was something distant and aloof about this guy that irritated Vince. You asked a question and you got a stiff, formal reply and nothing else. He wasn't going to volunteer anything.

'Peter!' A man's effeminate voice came from somewhere at the back of the shop.

'With a customer, Tim,' said Mr Aloof over his shoulder. And then Tim appeared, a camp individual in his early thirties with long, flowing blond hair and hipster jeans that Vince hadn't seen since the early 1970s.

Tim eyed Vince up and down and then looked at Peter.

'Mr Narraway here,' said Peter to Tim, 'is a friend of the Blattners. He's come to look over *the* shop.'

'Oh,' said Tim. 'Very upsetting. *Very* upsetting.'

Vince addressed himself to Tim. 'Did you know Lionel at all? At all well?'

Tim said, 'We used to pop in there all the time for odds and bobs, but I can't say we knew him well. He kept very much to himself, didn't he, Peter?'

Peter nodded.

Tim continued. 'He was always very polite and friendly, but we don't know anything about him. I'm sorry.'

'Were there any rumours going around after all this happened?' asked Vince.

'Why are you asking all these questions, Mr Narraway?' inquired Peter.

Vince figured he should low-ball it. 'Because, simply, the police have closed their investigation without turning up anything. And the family need to know why. That's all.'

'I see,' said Peter as he straightened his tie.

'I can tell you there were no rumours linking him with the scene here,' whispered Tim, rolling his eyes and grinning.

'The scene?' inquired Vince.

'Yes, the *gay* scene,' volunteered Tim.

Vince kicked himself for not being quicker on the up-take, for not realising what Tim meant.

'Did we hear any other rumours, Peter?' said Tim.

Peter looked at Tim for a moment and thought for a couple of beats before saying, 'You're the one with a better ear for gossip and rumour, dear.'

Tim shot a look at Peter and then turned to Vince and smiled. 'I mean there were silly rumours, like the Mafia did it, but that's about all. However, a lot of people thought he had been mistaken for someone else.'

'Who?' asked Vince.

'Well,' continued Tim, 'they never said who. Just some-one else. It was never specified. It was the only way they could make sense of what had happened.'

Vince wondered if the two of them lived above the shop, whether they had been here the night it happened.

'Afraid not,' said Peter. 'We live in Cliftonville. We just use upstairs for storage.'

'I see,' said Vince.

There was nothing Vince was going to get from these two because there was nothing they knew. Nonetheless, he gave them his mobile number on the off-chance.

Vince thanked them and left the shop just as a rain shower appeared from out of a seemingly clear blue sky.

After changing into dry clothes back at the hotel Vince decided it was time to investigate the attic. He moved a chair across to the centre of the room and stood on it. Reaching up with both hands he pushed the cover up and slid it across until the darkness of the void was exposed. He then stepped down, opened the alloy ladder, extended it to full length and placed the upper end against the wooden frame set within the ceiling.

Taking the Mag-Lite torch, Vince ascended the strong but rickety ladder and peered into the darkness. He switched the torch on and looked about – a large empty loft apart from several water tanks but, most importantly of all, the area surrounding the entrance and extending over to the tanks was boarded above the joists. Perfect.

Vince climbed down the ladder, collected the expensive sleeping bag and the kip roll and then went back into the loft.

He laid the roll down one side of the entrance and put the bag on top of it. Then he pulled the ladder up, lay on top of the sleeping bag and placed the square wooden cover back in its original position, except that now he put a carton of Marlboro in the gap at the corner to prevent it closing fully.

Lying on the sleeping bag he now had a view across from the door of the room to the foot of the bed. If anyone was to enter he'd see them right away, and they'd never think of looking for him above. He'd fluff up the cheap sleeping bag and put that under the bedclothes of the hotel bed. That way any visitors would think he was there, in bed.

So that's that sorted.

Later that evening, after grabbing a meal downstairs in the restaurant, Vince dialled up the copper again and he answered: 'Hello? Terry Aveling here.'

The voice sounded young and friendly, and almost eager.

'Terry?' said Vince.

'Yes.'

'This is Vince Narraway. I got your number from Wally, the reporter.'

'Oh, Wally. Yes. Be careful what you say.'

'I will. We should meet up.'

'That shouldn't be a problem, Vince.'

'When are you free then?'

'I'm really tied up for the next day or so…here…at work. Mmmmh…how about Sunday? Sunday lunchtime?'

'That's fine with me. Where?'

'You know the railway station?'

'Yeah.'

'By the entrance. About 12.30?'

'Perfect.'

'There's a quiet pub round the corner we can wander off to.'

'Got you.'

'I'll have a copy of the *Mail on Sunday* with me. So you know it's me.'

'Good. Until then.'

'Until then.'

Vince then dialled up Sid. The phone rang a long time before he answered it.

'Who's that?'

'Me. Vince.'

'How you doing? Got any answers yet?'

'No.'

'Well, at least you're still alive. That's something.'

'Sure is.'

'No whispers or anything?'

'No, but give me time. I'm going to shake something from the trees.'

'You are?'

'Yeah. If I'm not going to be able to find them, then all I can do is wait for them to find me. Let them make the first move.'

'You need some extra muscle down there? Ain't a problem.'

'I can move swifter on my tod. I'll shout if it gets moody.'

'Do that.'

'I will.'

'*Ciao*, baby.'

'*Ciao*.'

Vince pressed the END button and stared across at the ladder and the loft space. He could really do with a good night's kip in a bed, but that was now a luxury he couldn't afford.

It's loft time.

6: On the Bean

VINCE HAD A FITFUL NIGHT in the attic and didn't fall
soundly asleep until about 5 a.m., consequently he didn't
arise much before noon.

After showering and grabbing a couple of cups of coffee
and a Danish pastry in the hotel lounge he wandered
around to his car and collected the maps he'd left in the
glove compartment.

He unfolded the Margate street map and spread it over
the bonnet of the car. He checked the address of the dye
works and located the street – over the back of the railway
station (though the works themselves were not marked).

It wasn't worth driving, the weather was better for
walking – it was bright and sunny though the wind was
very fresh.

Vince walked down past the harbour and along Marine

Terrace and then took a left after the monstrous tower block, then under the railway, then he was there – Station Terrace, a bleak cul-de-sac with a terrace of artisans' cottages standing on the left that was now empty and boarded up.

The opposite side of the road was merely rubble, all that remained of the facing row of railwaymen's habitations. At the end of the street were the gates to the now abandoned dye works, and hemming in the works and circling around to the back of the terrace were the rusty railway lines of a marshalling yard from which the goods had long since departed.

This was a backwater of Margate that never received any visitors. It was still and quiet and not even the sounds of the seagulls blessed this vista of what the architectural critic Ian Nairn would have described as 'industrial melodrama'.

The wind dropped.

Vince looked around.

He had an uneasy feeling.

He felt someone was watching him.

Vince turned 360 degrees, slowly, deliberately, looking for something.

Somewhere out there....

This wasn't just someone looking at him.

No.

Not some old man or kid or passer-by.

Something else.

Vince had a feeling of malevolence.

And it was near.

Very near.

Vince moved his right hand inside his jacket and rested his fingers on the .22 Walther and waited....

Then there was the deep and urgent sound of the warning horn from a non-stopping train high on the embankment as it raced towards Margate station with its rake of carriages.

A flock of birds arose from the rubble and dispersed in the sun's rays.

The spell was broken.

Vince let out a long breath, removed his hand from the pistol, relaxed his muscles.

The danger had gone.

Whatever it was had gone....

Vince was alone again.

He picked his way through the rubble, climbed an old wooden railway fence, and followed the track down towards the factory.

There it was: PRESCOTT & FORSTER'S THANET DYE WORKS.

Here was where Lionel had probably spent some time before his death and here was, without a doubt, where Phil had been gunned down.

All in the dye works.

At the back of the factory was a dock where goods wagons had been loaded and unloaded years ago. Now it was overgrown with bracken and weeds. Vince climbed up and walked along the raised area. There were rotting tin drums and wooden casks that at one time had held dye-stuffs and chemicals, there were wooden pallets that crumbled under your touch, lengths of tubing, packing cases, and even old telephone directories now three-quarters of the way to being pulp.

Vince continued down the back of the building and then around the side to the front that overlooked Station Terrace.

He appreciated the layout of the factory a little more now. It backed on to a marshalling yard from which further railway tendrils arced up and around to the dye works' own yard, and all this within the lee of the embankment that supported the main line train service through Margate.

Why was Lionel here?

What was Phil doing here?

Did the place have any significance beyond the facts that it was deserted and situated in a little-frequented part of this seaside town?

Certainly a good place to bring someone if you wanted to execute them.

Certainly a good place to entice and trap someone prior to offing them.

Little chance of being disturbed.

Little or none whatsoever.

All sorts of villainies could transpire here and nobody would be any the wiser.

Vince went through the main double-doored front entrance to the works and this opened on a lobby area that led to a number of offices ranged against the front elevation of the building.

Beyond the lobby was the ground floor factory area, dark and mysterious and illuminated by the occasional shaft of light beaming through a window. There were the dark shapes of now obsolete machinery and an acrid smell of some long-decayed and possibly noxious substance.

Vince soon found wide stairs that led up to the first floor. The ceiling here was lower and there were more windows, larger windows from floor to ceiling, and these gave a clear view across the floor. Whatever machinery had been here had been cleared out long ago, but footprints were visible on the parquet pine floor, ghostly outlines of clean wood with an aura of grease and grime.

Not a happy place for shoot-'em-ups in the daytime, let alone at night, thought Vince.

The second floor was much the same.

Vince wondered where exactly Phil had fallen, where exactly Lionel had been taken, but this was idle curiosity, it wouldn't answer a single question.

The police, presumably, had been over this place with an electron microscope. If they had found anything it hadn't helped them solve the crime.

Solve the *crimes*.

No.

Narrow wooden steps led up to the roof. There was a door at the top of them partially opened but jammed. Vince had to force it and then he was on the top of the building amidst the valleys and pitched roofs largely bereft of slates.

He walked to the parapet and stood there in the wind gazing across Margate to the sea. There was that tower block on the front, there Dreamland, and there the rise towards the old town, and there the harbour and the sea.

Gulls were circling high above, indifferent to humankind's dramas and passions being played out below.

There was a noise.

There was movement.

It was hard to say which came first if, indeed, they were not simultaneous.

From where?

Somewhere out front there, down Station Terrace.

Vince stepped closer to the parapet, the palms of his hands resting against the lichen-covered masonry.

There it was.

There.

Shooting and screeching forward.

A Mercedes estate. Faded white. About ten years old. Racing up the terrace and now taking a right and disappearing from sight under the railway bridge.

Where had it come from?

What was it doing here?

Why hadn't Vince noticed it?

It hadn't arrived while Vince was here. He would have heard it, even when he was inside the dye works.

Instinctively he figured there was some connection between this vehicle and the feeling he was being watched when he arrived.

There was cold sweat on Vince's forehead.

There was a sense of unease sweeping over him that he hadn't experienced since a child. The sort of unease that grabs a fistful of your innards and turns them a full circle.

That sort of unease.

That *exact* sort.

Vince walked back along the front, grabbed some fish and chips at the Primark, an eatery that overlooked the harbour, and then decided he'd wander up to Caesar's Massage Parlour on the Northdown Road and see if he couldn't shake some birds from the trees.

The joint was this end of Northdown Road and Vince thought it a pretty piss-poor operation.

Prior to being a massage parlour the premises had been a chemist's. You could still make out the name FREEMAN GRIEVE PHARMACISTS beneath a sheet of rectangular marine ply that had been whitewashed and fixed over the original sign. The words CAESAR'S MASSAGE PARLOUR had been rendered by some inexperienced sign-writer in serifed caps such as you saw on menus in cheap Greek restaurants (Greek, Roman, what's the difference?).

Black satin curtaining had been hung behind the plate glass of the front to give an air of mystery and luxury. A sign on the door said they were open seven days a week from midday to 2 a.m. and that they accepted all major credit cards.

Vince pushed open the door and walked in.

There was a small reception area with numerous arm-chairs, a coffee table displaying a wide selection of dog-eared girlie magazines, a small TV and video player, and on the walls posters of Miss August and her chronological companions, all showing their pink.

In the corner, behind a small desk, sat a heavy-set guy in his early thirties with long greasy black hair. He'd be the minder. The guy who made sure none of the punters got out of hand. He looked over at Vince and said with a hint of surliness, 'Can we help you then, *sir?*'

The voice was deep and uneducated and had inflexions that Vince took to be the local dialect.

'I've come for a massage.'

'Well then, *squire*, you've come to just the right place.'

Vince nodded. 'Who you got on today?'

'Who we got on today? We got the lovely Denise. That's who we got on today.'

'Uh-huh, not a choice then?' Vince replied.

The minder ignored Vince's question and, smiling at some private joke, leant forward, pressed the button on an intercom and said, 'Denise? There's a gentleman here.'

'Yeah. I'm just comin',' was the hollow and distorted reply through the intercom's tiny speaker.

The minder looked up, still smiling at some private joke, and indicated to Vince to sit down.

Vince shook his head and said, 'I'm all right standing.'

'Suit yourself. Anyway, that'll be £30, *sir*.'

'Uh-huh,' said Vince as he took three starched tenners out of his wallet and handed them over.

The minder stuffed the readies in his jeans pocket and said, conspiratorially, 'Any extras you have to negotiate with the masseuse. Right?'

'Right.'

'You wanna watch a video then?'

'What you got?' asked Vince.

'New one in today. Called *500 Oral Cum Shots*. Some great action.'

Vince said he'd pass for the time being.

The minder didn't appear to be a guy who would be forthcoming on anything. You'd probably have a tough time getting his true name out of him. No, he'd start with the girl Denise. See what she has to say.

Then Denise appeared. A cute brunette in her early twenties. She wore a lime green miniskirt that extended about two inches down her thighs and a lime-green top that had been cut just below her bra (a 36C?), thereby exposing her midriff.

She eyed Vince up and down and smiled, seeming to approve of him after all the weirdoes who usually wandered in. She wanted to know what Vince's name was? He told her.

'Follow me then, *Vince*.'

He followed her through a door and down a dimly lit lengthy corridor to a small bare room with a padded table in the centre, a chair, a washbasin and a plentiful supply of Kleenex.

'You want an assisted shower first?' asked Denise.

'No. Just a back rub would do me fine.'

Vince took his jacket and shirt off and threw them over the chair. He also took his shoes and socks off.

Denise said, pointing to the table, 'Lay down then.'

Vince lay on the table face down. He heard Denise unscrew a bottle and pour liquid from it which she rubbed into her hands.

He felt her fingers massage his shoulder muscles, working deep and in circles. It was a pleasant, relaxing feeling and Vince closed his eyes. He'd enjoy this for a while. He was always a sucker for back rubs.

Denise began working her way down his spine, alternating between her fingertips and the palms of her hands. There was a faint aromatic smell, not unpleasant, from the oil she was using.

The back rub was dissolving Vince's anxieties and tensions. This was the most relaxed he had felt in weeks.

The funny thing was, Vince thought, he'd never had a girlfriend, or a wife for that matter, who'd ever agree to give him a back rub. A proper back rub, that is. Sure, you got a couple of minutes and that was that. Like Julie. What did she say? 'I'm not indulging you. You go to a masseuse if you want a back rub.' Helpful, huh?

Vince heard Denise pouring more oil from the bottle and working it into her hands before setting about his lower back. She was kneading deep and hard and it almost took Vince's breath away, but even this was relaxing.

He was slipping away from consciousness when Denise's voice pierced the silence. A bored, defiant almost, question posed in broad vowels: 'You want any special services, eh?'

Special services? What was she talking about?

Special services.

Yeah, special services.

'What's on the menu, Toots?' replied Vince.

Denise then recited the menu of special services with the warmth and emotion of a Speak Your Weight machine. 'Hand relief is £25. Topless hand relief – £30. Oral is £40. Full intercourse – £50.'

Pretty appetising, thought Vince. Pretty damned appetising for anyone into robot sex. But what else did she have to offer?

'You mean kinky?' asked Denise.

'I don't know what I mean,' said Vince, his interest stirred.

'We do a bit of corrective if that's what you're after. Or I can get another girl in and we do Double Oral, that's £80.'

'I'll tell you what I want and I'll give you £50 for it.'

'What's that, then?'

'Some information.'

'*Information*?' she queried. He felt her fingers stop momentarily. She reacted as though she had been insulted. She doesn't mind giving a guy a good gobble, but *information!?* What did he take her for?

'Yeah, *information*.'

With the initial outrage over she composed herself and inquired, 'What sort of *information* you after then?' The word information being pronounced as though it were from some alien vocabulary.

'I want to know about a girl called Candy Green. You know her?'

There was a pause before she answered, a pause that was long enough to belie the reply that she gave, which was 'No.'

'I think you do, Denise.'

'I don't know anything. *Never* heard of *her*.'

'Yes you do.'

'Don't. OK? You got that?'

'What's the big secret? It won't go beyond the two of us.'

'I'm telling you. I don't know nothing. Never heard of her.'

'Never heard of Candy Green?'

'No. And that's final.'

Vince realised he wasn't going to get very far with this little darling.

'I'm just going to get something,' said Denise, petulantly.

Vince closed his eyes and waited for her to return. He was enjoying this back rub more than he'd expected. He'd have to treat himself to one on a regular basis.

Then Vince heard something. It was loud and urgent. He opened his eyes to see the door being kicked open and the minder taking seven-league steps into the room, his eyes aflame and bristling with some not very subtle aggression. Denise was following him.

'Right,' said the minder as he shoved Vince, 'get your clothes on. You're out of here, sunshine. Right now!'

Vince turned and swung his legs off the table as the minder shoved him again.

The minder had his fists clenched and Vince sensed he was aching for a bit of the old ultra-violence.

Vince reached for his shirt as the minder took a couple of steps towards him and shouted in his face, 'We don't like people asking questions here. Got that? They get into trouble.'

What dialogue! thought Vince. Straight out of a pulp crime novel.

At least let me get my shirt buttoned up, thought Vince. But the minder wasn't having any of it. He took another step towards Vince who then realised that like it or not this overweight asshole was intent on putting one on him.

'Give it him, Patrick!' shrieked Denise.

Two things immediately struck Vince about this remark. The first was, what's it matter to *her*? Why is she getting involved, egging him on? The second was, could this sleazeball of humanity really be called *Patrick*? Weren't Patricks slight guys with ginger hair and a devout belief in Catholicism? Well, some of them were....

Patrick indeed!

Vince chuckled to himself.

'What you fuckin' laughin' at then?' demanded Patrick.

'Let him have it!' instructed Denise.

Patrick took a further step forward.

Vince knew what to do. Knew exactly how to handle this. No problem. Sorted.

He took a step back which Patrick interpreted as submission, or, at least, a near-concession of defeat.

Then Vince held both his hands up at chest height with his palms facing towards Patrick.

Patrick saw this as abject submission. The poor fucker was holding up his hands to protect himself, this was defeat conceded all right. No rush, I can take my time giving him one. Coming in here and asking for information from our Denise. What sort of girl did he take her for?

And as Patrick relaxed his stand Vince flexed the muscles of his right arm and the palm of his hand shot forward and smashed into the minder's nose before the slimeball had time to realise what was going on. The manœuvre required little or no force, merely the straightening of the arm, yet it hit the minder with such power that it broke his nose.

Patrick stood there in disbelief trying to understand what had happened. The blood started gushing from his nose and the pain swelled up and he started groaning.

Then Vince's left hand shot forward and his palm went crashing into the minder's chin.

Patrick fell backwards and crashed against the wall.

He was still groaning as his consciousness ebbed away.

Vince turned and grabbed Denise by the arm. 'You're going to start making amends, sweetheart.'

She stared at him defiantly.

He pushed her against the table and said, 'Right. Candy Green.'

She shook her head.

'I'm going to ask you one more time. I want to know about Candy Green.'

Again she shook her head.

Vince reached forward, sunk his fingers down her fulsome cleavage and ripped the bra and top off her. Then he swiped her across the face with the back of his hand, not too hard but just enough to let her know he meant business.

She let out a strangled scream and fell to the floor.

Grabbing her hair he pulled her over to the unconscious Patrick. 'You want a nose like his?'

'No.'

'Tell me about Candy Green then.'

'She worked here for about a year. I didn't see much of her. We had a few drinks and that.'

'When did she stop working here?'

'About…uh…I dunno, six months ago?'

'Why?'

'Don't know.'

Vince sensed she did know. He grabbed her hair again and pulled her head back. 'Why did she stop working here?'

'Vicky Brown who runs the place didn't like having the police here asking questions. They were all over the place. She said it wasn't good for business.'

'Uh-huh. So why were the police here?'

'The geezer who was murdered. He used to come here.'

'What geezer was that?'

'I don't know. The one that got murdered. Had a shop.'

'Lionel Blattner?'

'Yeah, that was him.'

'So they came here asking questions about him?'

'Yeah. Told you.'

'Why were they asking questions about him, Denise?'

'Because he used to come here a lot. That's why.'

'Did you ever give him the treatment?'

'No. I used to see him here, but he only liked Candy. He didn't want any of the other girls.'

'So where's Candy now?'

'Don't know. Haven't seen her.'

'How do I contact her?'

'I got an address for her. She used to live in Arlington House.'

'Where's that?'

'You've seen it. The tower block down by the station. The big place next to Dreamland.'

'Uh-huh. What number?'

'Got it in my address book here,' said Denise as she reached out for her handbag.

She flicked through a small thumb-indexed notebook and read out a number to Vince. 'I don't know if she's still there. Might be.'

'What did you hear about this guy who was murdered, Denise?'

'What do you mean?'

'Were there any rumours about him? What he was doing here? Why he was murdered?'

'I didn't hear anything. You ought to speak to Vicky Brown. She might be able to help you. She's the madam here. Owns the parlour.'

'Where can I find her then?'

Denise pointed upward and said, 'The second flat above here.'

'Uh-huh.'

'She told us all that if anyone came around snooping we should tell Patrick. That was why I got him.'

'They don't like people asking questions here then?'

'No. Dead against it. Don't like it at all.'

Vince sat down and put his socks and shoes on and then his jacket.

He was just about to leave when Denise said, 'Didn't you say something about paying me for *information*?'

Vince stopped, turned to her and said, 'Paying you for information?'

'Yeah. That was what you said.'

'I would have done, had you not gone for laughing boy here.'

'Yeah, but I gave you the information!'

'Get real, Denise.'

'Cheapskate!'

Vince thought for a second, his good nature getting the better of him. 'Here's £20 though for a new bra and top.'

'Thank you *very* much!'

'And thank you.'

Denise grabbed the note as it fluttered to the floor and Vince exited.

Patrick started groaning again.

Denise turned to him and said, 'You can shut up.'

Silence then reigned at Caesar's.

Outside on the street Vince stepped back and looked up above the massage parlour. There were three further storeys that appeared to be flats.

At the side of the parlour was a door. Beside the door were three push buttons. Two of them had written names encased in plastic underneath and the third had the name in Dymo tape – BROWN.

Vince pushed the button and waited.

Nothing.

He pushed it again, stepped back and looked up to see if anyone had stuck their head out the window. Nobody.

Again he pushed it and waited.

No response.

No sign of movement.

He'd call back and see this Vicky Brown later.

The afternoon was drawing to a close but Vince thought he'd give Arlington House a whirl. See if he couldn't locate this Candy Green. See what she had to say for herself.

He walked casually back through the town, through Cecil Square and down the hill.

As he walked along Marine Terrace Arlington House was looming forebodingly above him as the salty winds came in off the sea.

It was quiet and there were few people about. The restaurants were open but empty. The seaside resort was winding down. The season was almost over.

There was an autumnal chill in the air.

Dusk was descending.

And now Arlington House.

And Candy Green?

Vince stopped on the pavement opposite the seafront and stared up at the tower block. A big, ugly, clumsy fucker of a development rising up and seemingly disappearing into the night sky. It looked like it was designed by the army for defence purposes, not by the local council for tenants.

He walked across the forecourt, into the lobby and took a waiting, empty lift to the fifteenth floor.

There was no one about. The block seemed deserted. He didn't even hear the sounds of kids or blaring record players. Just dead silence.

He found the flat and banged the door knocker a couple of times. And waited.

Nothing.

He banged again with force. The door rattled under the impact.

Then a voice from inside. A man's voice. 'Hold your horses. I'm just coming.'

Then the door opened. A bloke in his mid- to late thirties. Long blond hair, a moustache. Dirty jeans with paint flecks all over them. A black, long-sleeved T-shirt with an abstract design over which was printed the word GARBAGE. He looked at Vince apprehensively and said, 'I'm clean.'

'You're what?' asked Vince.

'Clean. Honest.'

Vince winked at him and said, 'I'm not who you think I am.'

'You're not the police?'

'No, I'm not. I'm down from London.'

'Uh-huh?'

'Some private business. Why don't you invite me in?'

The bloke was silent for a moment, then he said, 'I ain't gonna get any grief, am I?'

'No grief, I promise you.'

'Come in then. I'm Dave.'

'I'm Vince.'

'OK.'

Dave shut the door behind Vince and waved him down the corridor to the lounge at the end.

The lounge perfectly fitted the definition of that 1960s concept, a crash-pad: it looked like there had been a crash and it was padded. There were a couple of old sofa beds, some large scatter cushions and bean bags, a long low table (a coffee table it wasn't), rock posters on the wall, a stereo system and a TV and nothing else.

'Sit down, Vince. You want a coffee?'

'No thanks,' said Vince as he lowered himself on to a bean bag.

Dave flopped down opposite him and lit up a Gauloise. 'I been getting a lot of grief lately from the Old Bill.'

'Drugs?' said Vince.

'Drugs? Well, if you call *grass* drugs, yes.'

Vince nodded.

Dave continued. 'I mean I don't even deal. Just personal consumption. Nothing else. But they got it into their heads that I'm some major player down here. They've been turning me over on a regular basis. It gets to you after a while. Know what I mean?'

'I do.'

'What line of business you in then, Vince?'

'Low-profile organised villainy.'

Dave chuckled. 'Up in London?'

'Yes.'

'So what you doing down here then? And how can I help you?'

Vince lit a Marlboro and said, 'Candy Green.'

'Oh, *her.*'

'Yeah.'

'You didn't come all the way down here just for her, did you? Just to see her?'

'Not *just* for her, no.'

'What then?'

'Let's just say it's about something a bit larger,' said Vince.

'Got you.'

'Is Candy here? Is she your girlfriend?'

'Leave it out,' said Dave. 'I wasn't involved with her in any way. My wife left me about a year ago. So I was here alone and I rented out the bedroom to her. I dossed down in here.'

'Know her for long?'

'About a year. That's all. I met her through some friends up in the town. She was working as a waitress then.'

'Then?'

'Yeah, before she started at the massage parlour.'

'Is she still here?'

'Not in this flat she ain't. She scarpered a couple of months ago. She took all her stuff and upped and away. Owes me a couple of months' rent. Not even a goodbye or kiss-my-arse or anything.'

'You know where she is now?'

Dave thought for a moment and then said, 'She had this girlfriend called Vera over in Cliftonville somewhere. She might be there, but I don't know the address or anything. The other place you might try is the Tivoli Ballroom.'

'The Tivoli Ballroom? Why there?'

'She used to pick guys up there.'

'Where is it?'

'Up the top of Marine Terrace. You can't miss it.'

'Did you know she was on the game…uh, working in the massage parlour when you rented the room to her?'

Dave paused, lit another Gauloise and then said, 'I'd heard a whisper, you know? But, like they say, live and let live. As long as she didn't bring any of her *clients* back here, I didn't care.'

Vince felt that Dave was on the level. There were some more questions he wanted to put to him. 'Was she a local girl?'

'I think she came from Ramsgate.'

'Did she speak much about the job at the massage parlour?'

'We didn't speak much about anything 'cos we hardly ever saw each other. I was decorating during the day and being a barman at night. We used to say good morning or good night depending on the time of day as we passed each other outside the bathroom. That was about it.'

'She attractive?'

'Yeah, but a bit tarty.'

'Bright? Intelligent?'

'Artful, crafty, I'd say.'

'You hear anything about the murder investigation? Lionel Blattner, you know?'

'Lionel Blattner? The newsagent?'

'The very same.'

'The police interviewed her a few times about him because he used to go up there and she'd wank him off. That really freaked her out, being interviewed and that. The Old Bill came here a couple of times to see her and that's when they decided I was worth investigating, dope-wise.'

'She say much about Blattner?'

'He used to give her a good tip each time.'

'You know how the Old Bill found out about him going up there?'

'Candy reckoned one of the other girls tipped them off.'

'Anything else I should know?'

'I'd speak to that Vicky woman who runs the place if you want to know what went on up there, *if* she'd talk. She's as hard as old nails. I met her once. Not a pleasant bit of work.'

'You ever hear any rumours about Blattner? Why he was killed? Anything?'

'Just the silly stuff. The Mafia executed him! Stuff like that.'

'Perhaps they did?'

'You serious?' Dave laughed. 'Down *here*? The Mafia?'

'Yeah, I know. You got any theories then?'

'Him bound up like that. A shot through the head. Not local, is it?'

Vince knew he was right. It wasn't local.

Dave continued, 'I did think it might have had something to do with the massage parlour. They're a nasty lot up there, but they're not murderers. No way.'

Vince wrote down his mobile number in a notebook, tore the leaf out and gave it to Dave. 'If you hear anything or remember anything I might want to know about, give me a call.'

'You bet.'

Dave showed him out and they shook hands.

The tide was in and the sea was choppy as Vince walked along the seafront smoking a Marlboro. It was dark now and all the illuminations along Marine Terrace were lit. The place was more crowded now than it had been during the daytime.

Vince stopped up by the clock-tower and looked across. There it was, its name in flashing neon lights – THE TIVOLI BALLROOM.

Would Candy Green be there tonight touting for customers?

Vince ran the whole business of the massage parlour through his mind again. He was beginning to think it was a total red herring, that it had nothing to do with Lionel's murder. It was a side-track. A cul-de-sac.

So Lionel was a frustrated old bachelor who went for a weekly wank at some third-rate knocking shop. So what? He paid his bill there and that was that. He wasn't planning to take over the operation or close it down, was he? He wasn't demanding protection money, a cut of the action? No.

This massage parlour stuff is a non-starter.

Probably.

Very likely.

But, nonetheless, it would be useful talking to Candy Green and Vicky the madam. They were seeing a side of old Lionel that few others saw. They might have picked up something that could lead somewhere.

Might.

But that's supposing Lionel knew what was going on.

But Vince didn't think he did.

So where are we then?

In a loop?

Lionel's execution must have been as big a surprise to him as it was to us.

So that puts little Candy and Madam Vicky out the game again.

But what the hell, thought Vince, I'll wander over to the Tivoli and have a drink on the way home.

Vince crossed the street and walked up the steps to the ballroom. There was a ticket kiosk with the sign PALAIS DE DANSE and a lobby that resembled a 1930s cinema. Vince paid the £5 admission and walked over the deep carpet and through the swing doors to the ballroom itself.

The room was vast and belied the smallness of the entrance. A polished, sprung wood floor reflected the light from the chandeliers and from those curious multi-faceted revolving balls that bounced light in a thousand different directions.

Along the sides of the ballroom were tables and chairs where couples and groups sat drinking, laughing and watching the dancing on the floor.

There was a bar on the left and another on the right and at the far end was the bandstand, but there were no live players, just a guy with headphones playing records and wearing an evening suit slap bang in the middle. A DJ for the *Come Dancing* crowd.

Vince recognised the tune that echoed throughout the room. It was *Crazy Rhythm*. ('Recorded by Mr Isham Jones in April, 1935,' the DJ had announced seconds before Vince had entered.) The music came from large speakers suspended on the columns that surrounded the dance floor and the acoustics were clean, if a little hollow and reverberant.

The ceiling was elaborately decorated with mouldings and hidden lights. A *palais de danse* all right. Perfectly preserved from the day it was built. Early 1930s in aspic.

The bar on the left seemed to be where all the action was so Vince cut the corner of the dance floor and threaded his way through the tables.

'What can I get you, sir?' said a barman. He was in his early twenties with dark olive skin and black hair tied back in a pony-tail.

'A large vodka on the rocks, I think.'

'Certainly.'

Vince sat on a stool and looked around as the barman prepared the drink. There were a number of young girls by themselves between the bar and the bandstand, sitting, waiting, expectant. Any one of them could be Candy, thought Vince. Then again, any one of them could not be her either.

The barman put the drink down and said something, presumably the price, but Vince wasn't paying attention and just handed over a tenner.

Then Vince poured a little water in the drink and continued gazing about the room.

The barman put his change down on the counter and Vince said, 'I need your help.'

'Uh-huh.'

Vince felt the kid was streetwise, that he could speak to him.'I'm doing a little inquiry for a friend of mine. I need to talk to a girl who comes here a lot.'

The barman winked at him and said, 'You're talking a girl or a *girl*?'

'I'm talking a *girl*,' replied Vince.

'Plenty of them here. Take your pick.'

'This one's called Candy Green. Ever heard of her?'

'No. They change their names all the time though. Difficult keeping up with them.'

'Never heard of her?'

'Nope. But I'm the wrong person to ask. Talk to one of her sisters-in-arms. They might know something.'

'What do I do?' asked Vince. 'Wander over there and start chatting to one of them?'

'No, save yourself the trouble. Grab a table. Sit tight. They'll come to you.'

'Done,' said Vince winking at the barman as he slipped off the stall and ambled over to a table near the dance floor.

Vince sipped his drink, lit a cigarette, enjoyed the music and admired the dancers as they glided elegantly around the floor to the strains of *You Took Advantage of Me*.

The music ended and the DJ announced, 'Don't forget that the Modern and Rock Disco starts at 9 p.m. sharp when Jerry DeWald will have you rocking in your seats, in the aisles, and, most importantly, on the floor. But for those of you of a more traditional persuasion, we return to Mr Isham Jones and his rendition of *Sugar*. Take it away, Isham!'

The music began and then Vince sensed someone standing close behind him. He turned and saw a petite blonde girl in a tight-fitting silver dress that displayed a cleavage courtesy of a Wonder Bra rather than nature's own endowments. She had big lips that were bright red and she said, 'Would you like to dance...or something?'

'Why don't you sit down?' said Vince.

'Yeah, OK then,' she replied, 'and I'm Marilyn. What's your name?'

'Vince.'

'Nice to meet you, Vince. I used to have a friend called Vince...a long time ago.'

Vince eyed her over as she sat. Not unattractive at all. A nice direct manner devoid of any guile or pretence. It was hard to pinpoint her age. Early twenties? Late twenties or what?

She lit a cigarette and said, 'You been here long?'

'No, just got here.'

'What you doing here?'

'Here? In the ballroom or in Margate?'

'In the ballroom, silly.'

'Looking for something.'

'Aren't we all? What did you have in mind?'

'I need some information. You'll get paid for it.'

'I will?'

'You will.'

'What then?'

'You ever heard of a girl who does the ballroom here called Candy Green?'

'Candy. Yeah, I've heard the name here. I don't know her. Just heard the name.'

'You suppose any of your colleagues might know her?'

'Why do you want to know about her?'

'She's safe, don't worry. She knew someone who got murdered. I'm just making some inquiries on behalf of the deceased's family. That's all. I just need to talk to her. Nothing else.'

'You're not the police then?'

'No.'

'Hold on a jiff. I'll see what I can find out,' and with that Marilyn got up and high-heeled it to the other side of the bar where there were still some girls waiting for the johns to show up.

Vince finished his drink, went over to the bar and got another one, and returned to the table to the sound of *Dardanella*.

Marilyn returned a few minutes later with a piece of paper. 'I've got her address for you. I got it from Cindy. The black girl over there on the right.'

Vince looked across to Cindy. A tall elegant black girl, well dressed, with her hair in ringlets or whatever they call it.

'Does Cindy know her then?'

'*Knew* her. Hasn't seen her for a while.'

'Would she talk to me?'

'She says she doesn't know anything about her. Only ever saw her here. Nothing else.'

'How come she has her address then?'

'She asked her round once. But Cindy never went. She had it in her address book.'

Vince gave Marilyn a £50 note and took the piece of paper off her.

'You're very generous, Vince,' said Marilyn.

'Aren't I just,' he replied.

Vince unfolded the piece of white paper.

There was the address.

He read it.

It was the address in Arlington House. The one he'd just come from.

He laughed.

Marilyn wanted to know what was so funny.

Vince told her.

She laughed too.

Then Vince said, 'Are you any good at giving back rubs?'

'I've got strong fingers.'

'Want to come back to the hotel with me?'

'Sure. Where you staying?'

'The Trade Winds. Just up past the harbour.'

'OK, then. You want anything else?'

'No, just a back rub, really.'

'No problem.' Then, after a pause, she added, 'I'd love to, yes.'

I'd love to, yes. Vince repeated the words in his mind. There was something about the way she said it that excited him. Not sexually, but in some other way. Her eyes opened wide as she said it and Vince sensed a vulnerability that he found very attractive. *I'd love to, yes.* She seemed to say it as though she was addressing a lover rather than a client, not that Vince actually considered himself a client.

They left the ballroom and crossed through the park, where Marilyn took Vince's arm and snuggled up to him. He put his arm around her. She was all right, this Marilyn. A good kid, Vince thought. And genuine. Straight up genuine.

Marilyn had large innocent eyes and when she spoke to Vince she looked him in the face and Vince felt as though she was seeing beyond his eyes and into his soul. He thought only teenagers felt a *frisson* like this.

It was warmer now and the sea was calm. Far out were the twinkling lights of ships passing in the night. And there in the night sky a crescent moon. A Margate nocturne.

They reached Vince's room and he stripped down to his underpants and lay face down on the bed. Marilyn kicked off her shoes, hitched up her dress, and straddled him above his thighs.

'I haven't got any oil unfortunately,' she said.

'Don't worry,' Vince replied.

She had a healing, therapeutic touch. Much better than that scrubber's in the massage parlour. Marilyn had real soothing hands. Vince closed his eyes and let out a sigh of contentment.

Marilyn whispered, 'I can stay all night if you want.'

Vince thought of the sleeping bag in the loft and the ladder and the precautions he had to take and reluctantly said, 'We'll do it another night.'

'Why's that?'

'Because I might be involved in some trouble and I wouldn't want you to get caught up in it.'

'You know best.'

'Not often, but I do this time,' said Vince.

Marilyn left an hour or so later. Vince gave her another £50 note and she gave him her telephone number which he instantly memorised. He always did that with the numbers of girls he fancied.

7: Shadowlands, Dreamlands

THE POCKET ALARM CLOCK woke Vince in the attic at 10 a.m. He turned it off and went back to sleep for another hour.

He got up, showered and went down to the lounge for coffee and a hurried look through the front pages of the Sundays before heading out and along the front.

It was a very fresh morning and there were few people about, just thousands of seagulls that seemed to have descended upon the town from miles around. It's just like a scene out of that Hitchcock film, thought Vince. Spooky almost.

Halfway along the front opposite Marine Terrace the mobile rang.

'Hello?' said Vince

'Sid here. Hadn't heard from you for a while. Thought I'd give you a bell. See you were still in one piece.'

'I'm still in one piece.'

'Good. What you come up with then?'

'Fuck all, but I'm still digging.'

'Fuck all?'

'Fuck all, that's right.'

'I thought you were my number one investigator? Number one fixer and that?'

'I am, believe me.'

'But you've come up with *nothing* so far?'

'It's a slow job, Sid. You'll have to be patient.'

'You need more hands down there?'

'No. Not a good idea.'

'What then?'

'Just bear with me.'

'Perhaps some muscle would move it along?'

'Sid, *not* muscle. Just time and patience.'

'If you say so.'

'I do, Sid.'

'So you ain't had any *visitors* yet?'

'None…except for a cutie last night.'

'You be careful, son, where you dip your wick.'

'I always am.'

'I'll be in touch.'

'Good.'

Vince pressed the red button on the phone and ended the conversation. He looked at his watch. It was 12.25 p.m.

The station forecourt was empty except for a couple of parked cars and a couple of taxis.

Vince walked into the booking hall and spotted Terry Aveling right away. He was the only person there and he had a copy of the *Mail on Sunday* under his arm. Based on his voice, Vince had expected him to be shortish and powerfully built, but he was the opposite. About six feet two inches and painfully thin, with a slight stoop, and spectacles. Vince always prided himself on being able to identify coppers at 500 yards, but he'd never have guessed it about this geezer. He looked more like a college lecturer.

Terry was in his late forties and had a slightly down-at-heel aura to him. It wasn't his clothes, these were clean and new, rather it was his karma. A karma that exuded regret, disappointment and, possibly, failure too.

Vince walked up to him and extended his hand.

'You're Vince?'

'Uh-huh. And you're Terry?'

'I am.'

'You've driven down today, have you?'

Vince realised he meant driven down from London. He wasn't going to disabuse him of the idea. 'Right, I have. Where shall we go then?'

'There's a quiet little pub around the corner, off the Canterbury Road,' stated Terry. 'I'll go first. Follow me at a distance.'

Vince found the suggestion rather melodramatic and Terry sensed this for he added reassuringly, 'I'm well known around here. Two of us walking together in the open means we have a purpose with a capital P, whereas sitting in a pub – well, we're just having a drink. Psychology. Get my drift?'

'Your manor. You're the boss,' said Vince, conceding that Terry knew his own patch.

Terry nodded. 'Wait by the entrance here. Follow me when I disappear from sight over there.'

'Got you.'

Terry walked across the station forecourt at a leisurely clip, through the empty car park and disappeared behind a row of old houses.

Vince set off walking in a straight line to the point where he last saw Terry. When he got there he looked down the street just in time to see Terry take a left turn. He followed after him.

When Vince reached the main road, the Canterbury Road, he saw Terry on the opposite side some fifty or so yards ahead.

Rather than cross the road Vince decided that he could

shorten the distance between them if he remained on his
side of the road. So he quickened his pace and was soon
almost abreast of the copper who was still sailing along at
his leisurely amble.

Vince felt this was beginning...*was* like something out of
that Hollywood comedy, *Naked Gun*. He also began to
wonder whether Aveling wasn't a brick short of a load or,
indeed, as he'd heard one of Wally's friends say, a canary
short of a wharf?

Was the guy really for real?

He'd soon find out.

As Vince glanced across he saw Aveling turn down a
side street. Vince crossed the road and held back in order
to put some space between the two of them. Then he continued and ahead saw Aveling taking a left and vanishing
from sight.

Vince quickened his pace and arrived at the corner to
find he had lost Aveling, but there ahead he saw a small
pub overlooking the seafront. That must be it.

Good.

Aveling was standing at the bar just about to order
when Vince walked in.

'Fancy seeing you here, Vince,' said Aveling, acting as
though they hadn't already met.

Vince went with it. 'Just passing. Thought I'd drop in for
a quick one.'

'What'll you have?'

'Vodka on the rocks.'

'That'll be one lager and lime and a vodka on the rocks,
barman, please.'

The barman nodded silently.

Vince wondered again if this melodrama wasn't all
getting a bit out of hand, but he had no choice other than
to go along with it.

The pub was empty aside from a knot of teenagers in
the far corner and a couple of OAPs sitting by the door.
The chairs and tables were old and worn and the place

seemed like it hadn't been redecorated since the late 1940s. Vince sensed that even though it was on the seafront it was purely local trade that kept the place going. There were little or no attractions for the raucous day-trippers and holidaymakers.

Aveling paid for the drinks and led Vince across the room to a corner table by a fireplace that had been bricked up.

'Your good health, Vince,' said Aveling as he supped his lager.

'Cheers,' replied Vince sipping his vodka.

'I suggest we get business out of the way first,' Aveling stated.

Business? thought Vince. What's he rattling on about?

'By which I mean my fee,' continued the copper.

Fee?

Fee, oh yeah. Vince twigged what he was going on about. He meant his back-hander. His bit of bunce. His graft. The Nelsons. The spondulicks. Jack Dash. Yeah. But *fee?* Vince had heard it called many things in the past, but he'd never heard it dressed up like that before. Fee indeed! For professional services rendered, no doubt.

'What you got in mind then, Terry?'

'Two hundred pounds, I think, would do very nicely.'

Vince wasn't going to waste time arguing with the guy. Two hundred pounds was small beer by any standards. 'You're on.'

After looking around the pub Vince took out his wallet, removed four £50 notes and handed them to Aveling under the table.

Aveling's face broke into a big smile, just like a small kid who's been given a bar of chocolate.

'Very nice, Vince. Very nice indeed. I can see we're going to be good friends.'

'Uh-huh.'

'Now, if Wally put you on to me in connection with the little bit of trouble we've been having down here, I take it that you work for the brother of our late local newsagent here?'

'Correct.'

'As did Phil and Leo.'

'Spot on.'

Aveling nodded, sipped his lager again and took out a box of Panatellas which he offered to Vince. Vince shook his head and lit up a Marlboro instead.

'Where shall we begin?' said Aveling as he took the cellophane off a Panatella.

'What's happening with the Lionel inquiry?'

Aveling lit the Panatella, inhaled deeply, exhaled and looked Vince straight in the eyes. 'Nothing. Nothing, in a word.'

'Nothing?'

'*Nothing*. The case is still open, but there's nobody working on it. It came to a grinding halt. All possible avenues were explored, suspected leads followed up, crank calls investigated, and we ended up with nothing. All we can do now is wait. Wait for someone to come forward, wait for something to turn up. That's all. You know this anyway.'

'A big blank?'

'A big blank.'

'Let me ask you a couple of questions then.'

'Certainly, Vince.'

'Were there any theories or rumours going about? Any working hypotheses you guys had?'

Terry thought for a moment and then delicately flicked the ash off his Panatella into the ashtray. 'For any theory or hypothesis you need information, something to go on, something to begin with. In this case we had nothing. It wasn't robbery as he was found with money on him. Nothing that we knew about the man or could find out about him pointed to this being in any way connected with anything criminal that he might have done. So, given those circumstances, it was hard to come up with any theory. We had to dig around and see what we could find.

'Now, as to rumours. The seafront was buzzing with them, but each one was more outlandish than the last. You get them with every murder investigation.'

'What sort of rumours?'

'You know, he had all the unrecovered money from the Great Train Robbery under his bed. He'd secretly won the Lottery and had stashed £5 million away somewhere. He was an international drug dealer. A team of hit men had got the wrong fellow. All that sort of nonsense.'

Vince wanted to know about Candy Green and the massage parlour. What was that all about?

'One of the girls at the massage parlour was an informer. She'd been busted for drugs a couple of times and one of my officers developed her. It was useful having a set of eyes and ears in that establishment. She called us and said Lionel had been a regular visitor and told us about this girl Candy being the only one he went with. He'd been going there about six months. We had Candy in a couple of times but she didn't know anything.'

'Do you think I might be able to get something out of her you lot didn't?' asked Vince.

'She's got nothing to say. Blood out of a stone, I'd say. But you can try. Who knows?'

'Was any serious pressure put on her?'

'No. We had no reason to. There was nothing connecting her to the crime.'

'Did she have an alibi for the night it happened?'

'Rock solid on the face of it. She was at the massage parlour and then at some party. About half a dozen witnesses to corroborate it all. Seemed strong enough, but I don't know how it would have stood up in court.'

'You have an address for her?'

'Uh-huh.'

'Current?' asked Vince eagerly.

Aveling nodded a yes. He took out a small hardbound notebook from inside his jacket and thumbed through the pages. '16 Weatherlees. That's all one word. L – E – E – S.

In Sandwich. She's lying low there. Not on the phone.
Some boyfriend, I think. I'm not sure.'

Vince wrote it down in his diary. He'd come this far
trying to trace her, he might as well drive down to Sandwich on the off-chance.

'What about Vicky Brown then?'

'The madam, as it were?'

'Right.'

'We had her in too. She spends all her time upstairs in
the flat administering discipline and enemas to the local
gentry. She didn't know anything. She was only concerned
with the money.'

'In other words,' said Vince, 'the issue of the massage
parlour is a non-starter? Has nothing to do with what
happened?'

'I can't see that it did, can you? Another drink?'

'Let me get these,' said Vince. 'Same again?'

'Please.'

One moment Vince thought there was a connection
between the massage parlour and the murder and the next
he was convinced there wasn't. But something kept
returning him to the place. There might just be something
there.

When Vince returned with the drinks Aveling was doing
the crossword puzzle in the *Mail on Sunday*. He looked up
apologetically and said, 'Can't resist the old crossword
puzzle. Keeps the grey matter alive.'

Yeah, thought Vince, and I bet you play Scrabble too.

Vince handed Aveling his drink and said, 'Coming back
to the massage parlour. What did Lionel get up to there?'

'You mean sexually?' asked Aveling.

What on earth else could I have meant? thought Vince
as he nodded at the copper.

'Pretty straightforward,' continued Aveling, 'from what
we found out from *Miss* Green. Just hand jobs. Nothing
else. No touching, no anything. Lionel was, I think, a very
repressed individual.'

Vince suspected he was. That old Middle Europe Jewish background weighed heavily upon him. What was that old joke about a Jewish porno film? The definition of one? Five minutes of sex and fifty-five minutes of guilt. That was it. Vince smiled to himself.

'Tell me about the dye works now,' said Vince.

'That was our one major breakthrough. We thought it would lead us to something, but it didn't. It just petered out. But it did establish a location for Lionel between Mrs Spooner leaving the shop and the discovery of his body the next morning.'

Vince wanted to know more. 'How did you get on to it in the first place?'

'Lionel was wearing an old dark grey suit. You couldn't help noticing this light blue powder all over it, particularly down his left side. It hadn't come from the beach, so we reasoned, correctly, that he'd picked it up from wherever he'd been before. Forensic soon identified it as a dyeing pigment so we went around to the old Thanet dye works and we got a match.'

'Did you find anything there?'

'This particular blue pigment was only found at the back on the ground floor. There was evidence of the ground being disturbed there, so we concluded that that was where matey had been taken. We didn't turn anything else up. We took the place apart. We had teams crawling over it with magnifying glasses. We did everything we could. Nothing. Whoever was there knew what they were doing all right. Very careful.'

'Why was he taken there? Why do *you* think he was taken there?' asked Vince.

'You're making an assumption.'

'I am?' said Vince startled.

'You are. We don't know he was *taken* there, forcibly taken there. He could have gone of his own free will. He could have been *lured* there.'

'Was he?'

'How would I know, Vince? But the end result was the same for him. Exactly the same.'

'Why do you suppose he was shot there and not, say, at the flat or the shop? They wouldn't have been disturbed there, would they?'

Aveling scratched his chin and thought for a moment before answering. 'There are neighbours. It's a partly residential street. Somebody just might have seen or heard something. There are too many things to go wrong.'

'What about the dye works then? Anybody could have wandered in there. Anybody.'

'Not true,' countered Aveling. 'Young kids sometimes during the day out for a lark, but at night nobody. It's too far off the beaten track. We don't even find winos there or down-and-outs.'

'So why was he taken there?'

'Obviously, to be shot…to be executed.'

'Why do you say *executed*?'

'Because that's what it was, wasn't it? We both know that. I knew it the minute Wally got in touch with me and I found out about Sid.'

'So what's the answer?'

'The answer is that poor Lionel died as innocent as the day he was born. This was nothing personal, at least insofar as *he* was concerned. Lionel died because he was Sid's brother. This was a message to Sid.'

'From who?'

'You tell me,' said Aveling. 'You know Sid better than I do.'

Vince was silent. Aveling was merely telling him what he knew already. Indeed, what he knew even before he schlepped down to this fucking seaside resort and started nosing around.

Vince thought, after all this, I'm still on square one in this Snakes and Ladders game. I can't throw a six to get moving. Not even one fucking six.

The dye works. Vince's mind kept returning to the dye

works. Lionel, Sid's brother, was taken there. Harry, well, we don't know about him. Leo was shot in the hotel. Phil was shot in the dye works and, unlike Lionel, was found there too.

'Could it be,' said Vince as he rubbed his eyes, 'that Lionel was taken to the dye works because they wanted to do something before they offed him?'

Aveling warmed to the suggestion. 'Yes. Possibly. But what?'

'I don't know. But there was a reason. Otherwise they'd have just done it...wherever.'

'They wanted to put him through it before they sent him off perhaps? But there were no injuries to the body other than the head wound. That appears to rule that out then.'

'Mmm. There's got to be a reason. Then dumping him on the beach....'

'So he was discovered right away?' added Aveling.

So that was it. Sid's brother was taken there for a reason, and what that reason was we don't yet know, thought Vince. Phil knew about Lionel being at the dye works so it wasn't that difficult to lure him there. It also separated him from Leo and therefore made the job of dispatching them both easier.

There was no intrinsic importance in the dye works then. It was a means to the end.

'You've kept Sid out of this?' Vince asked rhetorically.

'I haven't volunteered anything and nobody upstairs has made any connection. I mean, they know he's got a brother called Sid but they don't know who exactly Sid is,' replied Aveling.

'OK,' said Vince, 'now what do you know about Lionel on the night of the murder?'

Aveling finished his drink and thought for a moment before answering. 'Mrs Spooner left the shop at, I believe, about 6.30 p.m. He would have locked up. She was the last person to see him alive. He didn't visit any of the local pubs, not that he was accustomed to, as far as we could discover. He didn't go bowling and he didn't take himself up to the massage parlour. The next we know of him is on the beach the next morning after, of course, the stopover at the dye works.'

That was it: Aveling hadn't told Vince anything he didn't know already.

'When you went over the shop and the flat the next day,' asked Vince, 'did you find any evidence that anything had been forced? Any door, window, whatever?'

'No. Nothing like that.'

Vince remembered what Mrs Spooner had told him about Lionel never opening up again after he had locked up: unless, of course, he knew you.

Did he open up to someone he knew? If so, who would that be?

'You haven't got my name and number on you, have you, Vince?' asked Aveling.

'Yes, why?'

'Could be dangerous for me. Tear it up. Your colleague, Phil, thank God, had committed it to memory. Otherwise things could have been very, uh, *awkward* for me.'

'I'll do that,' said Vince.

'Just in case something happens to you. We don't want another body turning up here...*and* with my name on it. The balloon would go up.'

'Consider it done,' said Vince reassuringly.

Aveling stubbed out his Panatella. 'Another eighteen months and I'm retiring. I don't want the boat rocked.'

Vince asked about the 'Margate Massacre' – the murders of Phil and Leo and the landlady and her guests in the hotel.

'That investigation fizzled out, thank Christ. It could have been difficult for me. Very difficult. They reckon it was two London wide boys trying to muscle in on the amusement arcades and the drug scene. Something like that. We wouldn't want them to think any different. Would we?' said Aveling as he winked.

'No, we wouldn't,' added Vince. 'I've got a further question. They knew where to find Lionel. He was a sitting duck. They knew Sid and the boys would turn up for the funeral, so picking off Harry was just seizing an opportunity that was presented to them on a plate. But what about Phil and Leo? How did they find out about them?'

Aveling shook his head. 'That's kept me awake at night.'

'Any ideas?'

'Who did they see when they were down here? Go over the same ground. Someone passed on the word.'

'*You* figure on that list,' said Vince.

'I know, but you'll have to look further than me.' Then Aveling stood up. 'You know where to reach me if you need me. Give me ten minutes before you leave. And don't hang around Margate longer than you have to. The sooner you're back in London the sooner you're *safe*. Know what I mean? And the sooner I'm safe too.'

Vince nodded and Aveling was gone.

He wasn't sure what to make of the copper. A strange guy and probably on the level, if for no other reason than he had a lot to lose in this game as well.

But was he?

Coppers are often funny people. You'd never know.

Vince sat there finishing his last Marlboro. His mind began to wander to thoughts of Wells-next-the-Sea, to late breakfasts and sea fishing, tending his garden, wandering down to the harbour in the early evening and having a quiet pint of beer. Stuff like that.

And he thought of Marilyn too. There was something very engaging about her. She lingered in your mind like a catchy tune.

And Wells-next-the-Sea.

Every day over was a day nearer to realising that.

Every day was.

It really was.

Thinking this was the only way he could keep going.

A few minutes later Vince was out on the seafront breathing in the salt air.

Aveling was nowhere to be seen.

Vince cleared his lungs and then walked down to the sandy beach. There were few people about. The sea was grey and churning. The gulls were high in the sky, endlessly circling, waiting, expectant.

Vince headed east along the beach. He could do with a walk and it would only take a few minutes to reach Marine Terrace and the front at Margate.

As he was passing the Nayland Rock Hotel and just after vaulting a sea groyne Vince had a sudden feeling that he was not alone, that there was someone behind him, following him. He threw a quick glance over his shoulder and saw some distance off a figure walking in his direction. The figure wore a long grey mac and had a stumbling gait.

The feeling was similar to the one he had felt at the dye works.

Vince continued on and then swung around to the right, heading for a set of steps that led up to Marine Terrace nearly opposite the tower block where Candy Green once lived.

When Vince reached the top of the steps he turned and gazed out across the sea while looking to the left with his peripheral vision. The figure who was heading in his direction suddenly stopped and looked away.

Vince wondered if he was getting paranoid or whether he was under surveillance. He lit a cigarette and continued staring out (two entirely natural activities given the time and place) while weighing his options.

Vince took a few more puffs of his cigarette and kept a watchful eye on the figure who was now walking along the beach in a direction parallel to Marine Terrace.

After flicking the cigarette, still lit, down to the sand Vince negotiated the heavy traffic across the road. He could legitimately stop every so often and look into the windows of the shops and arcades while throwing glances over his shoulder to see if the figure continued his pursuit.

Sure enough, the figure soon appeared at the top of the steps. He looked around, up and down the terrace, espied Vince and crossed over in a diagonal direction more or less aiming for where Vince was sorting through a rack of local postcards.

Vince continued on along the terrace and then ducked into an amusement arcade some doors up from Dreamland. Once inside he stood behind a flight simulator at the front that gave him a clear view out on to the street.

Vince observed and waited.

A minute or two later the figure appeared at the front and stopped. The guy was in his middle to late thirties, of medium build, with longish dark hair and a moustache. His eyes were sunken and his skin cadaverously pale. He looked like someone who had spent his life underground.

Vince exited the arcade and headed back along the front in the direction he had come. He turned left into the Dreamland approach and stopped by a licensed bar that was blaring out some song by the Carpenters. Over his shoulder he looked back up towards the front – there was the figure turning the corner.

No doubt about it. This sucker was trailing him.

And he'd obviously been trailing him since he left Aveling. Was Aveling, then, behind it? Or had the guy been on him since he left the hotel?

When had this begun?

Vince needed to buy a few minutes to sort his head out and decide what to do next.

He headed for a candy-floss stall and purchased a large stick of the wispy pink confection.

Vince grabbed a handful, rolled it into a ball and popped it into his mouth and observed, out of the corner of his eye, the figure standing some distance off behind a group of teenagers over by the dodgems.

Just standing there keeping an eye on Vince. That's all he was doing.

There was music coming from the nearby merry-go-round. A fairground organ or barrel organ playing that tune they always seemed to play, that tune that everyone recognises, yet no one knows the title of…*that* one (*Les Patineurs*, by Emile Waldteufel, aka *The Skaters' Waltz*).

The cadences and flourishes of the organ were punctuated by laughs, shouts and shrieks from the predominantly teenage and early twenties clientele of Dreamland, all of whom were self-consciously having a good time.

Vince munched the candy-floss and weighed his options.

Then he threaded his way through the rides, past the roller-coaster and the side-shows at a casual pace carefully making sure the shadower *didn't* lose him.

On the edge of Dreamland was a large car park given over to a street market with dozens of stalls selling clothes, household goods, car accessories, food and even books and records. Vince desultorily looked over the stalls and wondered if he couldn't execute his plan, the switcheroo, here.

No.

Too chancey.

Vince brought a coffee in a paper cup from a stall and then wandered over to a guy who had large boxes of CD records filed under different headings: MIDDLE OF THE ROAD, CLASSICAL, HEAVY METAL and so on. There were other classifications too, including JAZZ.

The jazz section had a lot of records by modern artistes Vince had never heard of and a lot of New Orleans revivalist stuff that he didn't care for, but here were some albums by Lester Young, including a CD of quartet recordings from the mid-1950s. And only £3 each.

Vince reached into his pocket for some loose change and shot a casual glance over to his right. There was the shadower by a corner stall feigning interest in digital wrist-watches.

After handing over three £1 coins and getting the Prez CD wrapped Vince continued on over the asphalt to the Belgrave Road exit from Dreamland.

Here he took a left to the seafront.

He wasn't bothering now to check his companion was in pursuit. He knew he was.

At the front Vince finished the coffee and threw the cup into a litter bin.

He was hungry.

But one thing at a time.

He realised then how to accomplish the perfect switcheroo *and* get something to eat as well.

Vince bought an *Observer* from a corner newsagent and then proceeded up Marine Gardens to the Hungarian restaurant he'd first visited with Sid and Leo when they came down for the funeral.

There were few people in the restaurant and nobody sitting in the window, so Vince grabbed a window seat and waited.

The shadower must have seen Vince enter the restaurant because he now crossed the street and entered the park behind the clock-tower. He walked up and sat on a park bench and made out he was admiring the view.

Vince saw all this from the corner of his eye as he was pretending to read the paper.

Pretty good so far.

The waitress arrived and after a quick look through the menu Vince ordered the *chicken paprikash* and a glass of mineral water.

No need to rush things now, thought Vince. I'll just take my time.

Vince skimmed through the *Observer* and then enjoyed the large plate of spicy chicken with rice. He thanked the waitress, paid her, left a handsome tip and then walked quickly to the back of the restaurant, past the loos and through the yard on to the back alley.

Turning left on the alley Vince walked with speed and purpose up to the High Street and then along to the back of the park.

A narrow passage ran from the High Street to the park.

Vince went down it and at the end he stopped. There across the grass and the ornamental flowerbeds was the shadower waiting for Vince to return from the loo or settling his bill or whatever it was he thought Vince was doing.

The guy was getting impatient. He got up from the bench and walked slowly in the direction of the restaurant. He stopped on the pavement diagonally opposite the restaurant and waited, pacing up and down.

He looked at his watch several times.

Vince moved forward out of the shadows.

The guy crossed the road and went up the steps to the restaurant. He poked his head in and looked around. He then realised that Vince had gone, but not that a deft switcheroo had been completed and that *he* was the one now being followed.

Vince retreated into the doorway of a casino.

The shadower hurried back across the road and through the park.

Vince gave him a thirty-second start and then stepped out and began following him.

Crowds had appeared from nowhere and it was difficult initially for Vince to keep the guy within sight, but he kept the gap constant and stuck with him.

It was obvious that the guy did not suspect for a moment that he was now the quarry. He just continued on along Marine Drive and never once looked back. This little sucker isn't as experienced as he should be, thought Vince. If you lose your prey you better make very certain the tables haven't been turned. This guy hasn't taken the most elementary of precautions.

Vince followed him past the harbour and up the hill to Fort Crescent and then down a side road where he stopped. The guy searched in his pockets and produced some car keys with which he unlocked a white Mercedes estate.

A white Mercedes estate.

Vince thought back to the white estate he'd seen at the dye works. Was this one and the same?

Looks like it.

But then two other facts hit Vince like a shit monsoon.

The first was that *his* car was parked opposite, and the second was that Trade Winds was just around the corner.

The balance of the evidence seemed to suggest not that the guy had picked him up when he met Aveling, but that he had followed Vince from here, the hotel, to the meeting.

What was the alternative?

The alternative was that it was pure coincidence the guy was parked up here by the hotel.

And that seemed very unlikely.

If Aveling had tipped him off the guy wouldn't park here and walk all the way down to the station, to that pub.

No.

Most certainly not.

He'd been followed from the moment he left the hotel that morning.

The engine started and a few beats later the Merc pulled out into the street.

Vince took out his notebook and noted the registration number.

A face and a reg number.

Something to go on at last.

Something to start the ball rolling.

A beginning.

Yeah.

8: Hornin' In, and Some

VINCE GOT BACK TO THE HOTEL and after ordering some coffee from room service gave Sid a bell on his mobile.

'Sid here.'

'It's me.'

'Give me five, old son, I'm just having a bit of fun and games down with Barbara. I'll call you right back.'

'Got you,' said Vince, and then he pressed the red disconnect button.

So, Sid was down with that old – correction, *young* – slag in St George's Square. He always had one or two on the go. Vince didn't understand what Sid saw in these giggly, flibbertigibbet young tarts. Beautiful bodies, yeah, but at what cost? A one-night stand perhaps, but *regularly*?

The coffee arrived and Vince poured himself a large cup of black into which he put three sachets of brown sugar.

He lit a cigarette, took a couple of puffs and then immediately put it out.

He'd have to sort out what was going on. Decide what to do next.

Talk it over with Sid.

Then he nodded off to sleep.

About twenty minutes later the mobile woke him up. It was Sid.

'What you got for me then, eh, Vince?' asked Sid.

Vince said, 'First off, I've got a car reg number I want checking out. I want the name and address and I want it pronto, so I can get on to *them* before they get on to *me*. Right?'

'What's the number?'

Vince spelt the reg out twice then, 'I was followed today. In fact I think I've been followed on other days too. I'm not sure. But that's the number.'

'I'll get on this right away,' said Sid, 'but I may not have it until tomorrow morning. Depends who's about. Know what I mean?'

'Yeah, but chase it.'

'Sure thing. Anything else worth reporting?'

'I saw the boy in blue today, Aveling.'

'Oh, him. What's he got to say for himself?'

'Fuck all, but he gave me a useful address and put me right about a couple of things. In fact I thought he might have fingered me to the guy who was following me, but I'm not so sure now.'

'Why's that?' asked Sid.

'Because…well, I thought I was followed after the meet with him. But this geezer who tailed me was parked up by the hotel here, so I'm thinking – maybe he followed me *to* the meeting. I don't really know. I got to look into it a bit more. Find out the strength. You with me?'

'Yeah.'

'The thing is someone down the line put out the word. Said I was in town. I've gone over the same ground as Phil and Leo. There's someone broadcasting what's happening.'

'Any ideas who?'

'As I said, I thought it was the copper this afternoon, but I'm uncertain now. Got to look into it.'

'Anything else?'

'No.'

'You take care then, Vince.'

'Don't I always?'

'You do.'

'Bell me as soon as you got the name and address.'

'I will.'

Vince hung up and closed his eyes again. Then he opened them wide. He couldn't afford to fall asleep on the bed, he'd have to move up to the loft.

An early night.

And a pity he couldn't give Marilyn a bell.

A real pity.

A noise. A foreign noise. Something out of the ordinary. A click or a spring or something.

A strange noise.

It was there and then it was gone.

Wait.

Wait.

Listen.

There it was again.

A muffled, metallic click.

Wait.

Listen.

Click.

What was it?

And again – click.

Then silence for what seemed like a geologic epoch.

Deadening, deafening, suffocating silence.

Anything but golden.

Anything.

Vince moved his arm so his wrist-watch was just above

his face. With his right thumb and forefinger he pressed the ILLUMINATE button. The liquid crystal display declared the time to be 04:31:22.

A.M., that is.

Vince continued listening.

He looked at the watch again: 04:31:42.

Still silence.

Another metallic click.

Vince waited, the stuffy, dusty atmosphere in the loft invading his nostrils, making him want to sneeze.

Wait.

Another sound.

A different sound.

The door to the room was being opened.

Couldn't be anything else.

Vince reached across and took the .22 Walther from the holster. He released the safety switch – one in the chamber and five in the magazine. If he needed more than that to defend himself then it was foregone that he was dead meat.

He rolled on to his side and peered under the loft hatch.

He could see the bed to the right, illuminated by a shaft of moonlight, and he could make out the door to the left, just about.

He could hear the door slowly opening but it was difficult detecting any movement.

He waited.

The door opened further.

And then – then, *suddenly* – someone threw a jumping-jack firecracker into the room. A muted firecracker. And one that didn't seem to jump about.

Put-put-put-put-put-put.

Put-put-put-put-put-put.

Vince could smell it now as the smoke spiralled up to him. A heavy, acrid gunpowdery smell as thick as cigar smoke.

A firecracker so he thought.

But it wasn't a firecracker Vince now realised.

It was the raking burst-fire from a silenced automatic weapon.

The bullets were ripping into the bed and ripping into the bedside cabinet and now a few stray projectiles crashed through the windows, shattering the glass into a million shards and pieces.

And then silence.

The gunman had gone.

Vince waited a couple of beats to make sure it was all clear, but then alarm bells began ringing. Fire alarm bells. The cordite smoke had tripped the smoke detectors on the hotel's fire alarm system. It'll not only be the Old Bill swarming all over the place, but the fire brigade too. Not to mention the other guests....

Vince hurriedly got dressed, packed all his things in the case and rolled up the sleeping bag. He had to vanish and vanish quickly. Had he left anything down in the room? His toothbrush, yes. Anything else? He couldn't remember. But certainly nothing important. Fuck it anyway.

He moved rapidly over the joists through the attic and let himself out on to the roof through the skylight.

It was a cold, moonlit night.

Margate was twinkling at his feet.

Another nocturne.

He edged swiftly along the parapet over the adjoining houses to a hotel at the end of the terrace. This hotel had a metal fire escape down the back, and it was not difficult for Vince to lower himself on to it.

Far off there was the sound of a police siren. It was heading up here in the direction of the Trade Winds Hotel. Then the bells of the fire tender. Jesus! All of Margate was going to turn out for this, or so it seemed.

Vince had made sure that he could never be traced. He'd paid the hotel in cash, had false ID and had left nothing that could connect him with the visit.

The only snag could be someone turning up at the hotel

and asking for him...in person. Giving his name.

But who's going to do that?

Who's then going to connect him with the man who never was in Room 26?

A bit iffy, but nobody, he hoped.

So, probably, nothing to worry about on that score.

But what now?

What about right now?

What are the options?

Kip down in the car? No. Too suspicious. If any of the Old Bill are floating about Margate doing street-to-street searches they're going to ask a few questions to anyone having forty winks in a parked car at this time of night.

Drive out of Margate, park up somewhere in the country where it's deserted and have a sleep there? No, same objections and, besides, the police might be stopping anything that's moving around now.

Too late to check into another hotel. Much too late.

So what's left?

Not a lot.

Uh-huh.

That leaves just one thing. A night out on the beach.

Vince descended the fire escape down the back of the hotel and found himself in a walled garden.

There were several police sirens now. One of them sounded as though it was just up the street.

A wooden door at the end of the garden was secured merely with a bolt on the inside. Vince slid the bolt and found himself looking up and down an alley. To the left would lead up to Fort Crescent and back in the direction of the Trade Winds. Forget that. To the right? No alternative. Got to go in that direction.

Vince hurried along the alley and counted on the fact that he had probably five or more minutes to make himself scarce in the neighbourhood. It would take the Old Bill that long, at least, to figure out what was going on.

The alley ended in a narrow street of further hotels.

Vince crossed to the other side and headed down the hill. Sirens could still be heard in the distance.

Vince now recognised where he was. In the old Market Square. It was deserted. He kept in the shadows of the south side and was soon at the end and overlooking the sea.

Vince peered round the corner in each direction. No police cars, no cars, no pedestrians. Nothing. All clear.

It's now or never.

He walked swiftly across the road, over the pavement, along and down the steps to the beach.

Safe.

Better to kip here, in the lee of the sea wall, thought Vince. I'm not going to be seen by anyone up above.

So, he unrolled his mat and sleeping bag, had a piss against the wall, and then snuggled down for what remained of the night. It was icy cold now but the sleeping bag soon got him warm.

Vince fell asleep thinking that it doesn't pay to skimp on things like sleeping bags.

It really doesn't.

It was the light spots of rain on Vince's face that woke him. Light, cold spots of rain.

Vince opened his eyes to a Sahara desert of sand and, beyond, a turbulent dark grey sea. In the foreground was a mongrel dog, black and white, sniffing about and not quite knowing what to make of Vince's presence.

Vince turned to make sure the bag with his belongings was still there, wedged between him and the concrete sea wall. It was…thank God.

And what about last night?

He ran through the events that had resulted in him spending the night on the beach.

Totally un-fucking-believable…almost.

Yeah.

And what time is it?

8.10 a.m.

Vince was tired and wanted to go back to sleep, but it would be tempting providence to spend any more time here. And the rain was getting heavier.

He wriggled out of the sleeping bag, rolled it and the mat up and then climbed the steps to the front. Not many people about. Everything looked pretty quiet and peaceful.

Vince headed up to Fort Crescent and down the side street to his parked car. He drove back through the town and took a left down Belgrave Road. He'd noticed there were some very cheap b&b places in this locality and he wanted to check into one, get some breakfast, get some sleep and lie low for the rest of the day.

The Nookery Private Hotel fitted the bill perfectly. It looked run down with paint peeling from its name-plate fascia and an unkempt front garden. A flickering neon sign in need of repair advertised VAC — CIES.

Mrs Botherwick, a stout woman in her early sixties with dyed blonde hair and a fag in the corner of her mouth, welcomed Vince aboard. He could have her best room, the large one at the front just above the entrance. ('You can even sit out in the sun on the balcony if you want, luv. That's if we have any.')

Yes, she said, you go and settle in and I'll do you a nice big breakfast fry-up. Vince explained he had just driven down from Bristol and that he was looking at houses as the aeronautical company he worked for was relocating him.

'How interesting, dear. How *very* interesting.'

After breakfast and a shower Vince hit the sack and slept till the early afternoon when the mobile woke him up. It was Sid.

'How you feeling, son?'

'Fine, Sid. Just fine,' replied Vince who couldn't summon the energy to explain what had happened last night.

'That Merc reg number. I got a name and address for you.'

'Shoot,' said Vince as he reached across to the bedside table for his notebook.

'Fellow by the name of Leonard Henry Tipper. That's
T – I – P – P – E – R. Got it?'

'Uh-huh. The address?'

'Basement Flat, 33 Percy Street, Ramsgate.'

'Thirty-three?'

'Yeah, that's it. You want me to see if we can find out
anything about him?'

'Yeah. See what you can do. And I'll see what I can do
this end.'

'You're on.'

'Speak to you later.'

'Right, Vince.'

Vince dialled 192 on the mobile and asked for Tipper's
number. He was listed all right. Vince wrote the number
down in his notebook.

He sucked the end of the pencil and then wrote the
following on a fresh page:

> *See Candy Green*
> *Check out Tipper*
> *See Aveling re. Tipper & following on Sunday.*

It wasn't wise going out and about today. More prudent
to lie low. Get up early tomorrow. See what's happening then.

A new day.

As it was Vince didn't wake until just after 9 a.m. and by
the time he had showered and had breakfast it was 10.30.

He left the hotel and casually walked around the block
and along the seafront to ensure there was nobody trailing
him. There wasn't. He was on his lonesome today.

Then he drove down to Eaton Road and headed south
on the Ramsgate Road through the undulating hinterland
of the Isle of Thanet. The sky was cloudy and overcast and
there was a strong promise of rain.

Vince pulled over on the A254 just short of the high
railway viaduct in Ramsgate and checked the street map

for Tipper's address. It wasn't too far ahead. Just a few
turnings up the hill on the left.

He put his dark glasses on and continued driving, parking a few turnings away from Tipper's address.

Percy Street was a drab late-Victorian street of terraced
houses with open basements. The area was too run-down
even for the cheapest of b&b places and, probably, too far
off the beaten track as well. Fords, Vauxhalls, a couple of
small commercial vans and an old BMW were parked on
either side of the street, hardly any under ten years old.
But there was no sign of the white Merc estate.

Tipper's basement looked more run down than most.
There were a couple of metal dustbins and several black
refuse bags arrayed to one side of the front door that looked
like it hadn't had a lick of paint since the last Coronation.

The curtains were pulled on the window to the left of
the door so it was impossible to see in. The curtains and
the window looked grimy and greasy. Tipper, whatever
else he might be, wasn't a sunshine and fresh air freak.
Neither was he house proud.

Vince walked down to the end of the street and took a
left to see if there was some back way to the basement.
There wasn't. No alleyway or anything. The gardens
backed on to those in the parallel road.

Vince dialled up Tipper's number on the mobile to see if
he was in. The ringing was answered, but by an answering
machine: *Thank you for calling. This is Lenny Tipper's answering machine. I'm sorry I can't take your call right now, but do
please leave a message. I check the messages regularly even when
I am away from the machine, so I should be able to get back to
you quickly. Please leave your name, your number and the time
of your message. Thank you.*

It was an out of London accent. Somewhere in the
country. It was a colourless voice, yet there was something
to it. Some of the words were pronounced with just a little
too much attention to the vowels. Theatrical, thought Vince,
and perhaps even camp.

So who is Lenny Tipper and what's he all about then?

Vince walked back to the basement and wondered whether it might be worth checking with the neighbours? See what they had to say.

He climbed the steps above the flat and pushed a couple of doorbells. An arthritic old woman, almost bent double, answered the door.

'Yes?'

'Hi, I'm an old friend of Lenny Tipper's. I was wondering if you knew where he was?'

The woman stared at him quizzically and said nothing.

'Lenny. Down in the basement. I'm a friend. You know where he is?'

'Ain't he in?' she replied.

'No, he isn't.'

'Dunno. He comes and goes at all hours. I'd put a note through his door if I was you.'

'Yes, I'll do that. Thanks,' said Vince.

Fat lot of good that was.

Tipper can wait till later, thought Vince.

He returned to the car and headed out of Ramsgate, then south down the Sandwich Road, through Pegwell Bay and past the River Stour estuary. The tops of the vast cooling towers of Richborough power station on the right were seemingly lost in the rain clouds that had suddenly appeared.

A mean, heavy rain started falling.

Vince reached Sandwich and stopped by a pub that faced the river. He checked the map for Candy Green's address and found it was on the south side of the town, some way past the railway.

It took about ten minutes to get there through the rain and through the traffic works that blighted this little ancient town.

The road was a crescent of pre-war council houses, shabby, grey and uncared for. Gardens were overgrown and several of them sported abandoned washing machines and fridges as centrepieces amidst the long grass, and weeds.

Candy's house had no front garden, or, rather, what was the front garden had been entirely concreted over and now a rusting wheel-less Ford Capri sat on jacks waiting for remedial attention.

Vince parked outside the house and went up to the front door. The bell push was hanging off so he gave the knocker several bangs.

Then there was movement inside. He could see something through the frosted glass. And then the sound of a slammed door.

A dark-haired girl in her early thirties wearing a purple shell suit answered the door. She was drying her hands on a pink towel. She had small eyes that squinted at Vince. She didn't say anything. Vince had to make the first move, after all, *he* was knocking at the door, not her.

'I'm sorry to trouble you,' said Vince, 'but is Candy Green here?'

The woman continued staring at Vince.

Vince thought of the old crone back in Ramsgate. Is there some local congenital Kentish difficulty about answering questions down here?

'Candy Green. Is she here?'

The woman was silent for a moment and then said, 'Who shall I say is here?'

Should Vince give his real name or what?

'Tell her I'm Vince. I'm a friend of a friend.'

'You hold on,' said the woman as she closed the door and went back inside.

Vince stood as close as he could to the front door so as not to get wet, but the rain was driven and it lashed against him.

Then the door opened again.

A girl in her late twenties with hair dyed orange and wearing white lipstick. Her eyes were big and dark. She had a black leather skirt on and a dark T-shirt on which was printed the word USELESS.

'Yeah?' said the girl.

'Are you Candy Green?'

'Who are you then?'

'Vince. I'm a family friend of Lionel Blattner's.'

'What you knocking here for?'

'I just wanted to ask you a few questions.'

'I've already answered lots of questions. The police. Everyone.'

Vince smiled and in his syrupiest voice said, 'I know. It's just that I'd like to ask you a few myself. It won't take long.'

Her eyes wandered up and down Vince before she asked, 'What's in it for me then?'

Vince twigged what she meant. 'Fifty pounds enough?'

'Seventy-five's better.'

'OK.'

She stared at Vince in silence. After a few beats Vince realised she was waiting to be paid now.

Right *now*.

Vince took out his wallet, riffled through the notes and gave her a £50, a £20 and a £5. She looked at them carefully to ensure they weren't fake and then stated, 'We can't talk here.'

'I've got a car. Perhaps we can drive to a pub or something?'

'We'll do that. Yeah. Hold on. I'll get my coat.'

She closed the door, leaving Vince on the doorstep once again.

He waited...and waited.

And continued waiting.

He banged on the door several times.

The woman eventually answered it and looked at him as if to say, You *still* here?

'Where's Candy? I'm waiting for her.'

'Candy? She went out the back.'

Vince pushed past the woman and stomped down the corridor and through the kitchen to the back garden which opened on to a sea of allotments. No sign of Candy. He turned to the woman. 'Where she gone?'

'I told you. She went out. Was in a hurry.'

'She upstairs then?'

'No, she's *gone,*' said the woman. 'I told you.'

Vince wasn't sure whether to trust the woman or not. He pushed her out of the way and over her shouts ran up the stairs and checked the two bedrooms and the bathroom. No Candy there.

Vince kicked himself. How could he have been so stupid? How could he have been? Handing over the money like that? Letting her go back into the house. What a fucking idiot. Jesus!

The woman was shouting at Vince to leave the house.

Vince came down the stairs and said to her, 'When you see her again, tell her I'll be back for the £75 she just conned off me.'

'Seventy-five pounds!' said the woman. 'You gave her that!'

'I did.'

'Perhaps she'll be able to pay her rent now.'

'Not with my money, she won't. I want it back.'

The woman was silent.

'How long has Candy been staying here?' asked Vince.

'About six weeks or so,' said the woman. 'She helps out with the rent and that when she can.'

'Uh-huh. Is she a friend of yours?'

'No, not really.'

'How come she's staying here then?'

'She's a friend of my sister up in Margate. She asked me to take her in for a while.'

'I see. Who's your sister?'

'Vicky Brown. She's a *very* successful businesswoman, she is.'

Yeah, she certainly is, thought Vince, she's made a nice couple of bob wanking off old men and giving them damned good hidings.

'Good,' said Vince as he showed himself out.

He ran back to the car through the driving rain, fumbled with the keys, and got wetter still. He started the ignition and shot down the road in anger and frustration.

No use hanging about Sandwich waiting for that little strumpet to show up. No.

Still, we know where to get hold of little Miss Candy now, don't we?

Pay that Vicky Brown a visit.

She'll know. She's keeping tabs on her.

A bit of pressure on Miss Brown and she'll soon cough.

That can wait.

Now what?

Lenny Tipper, yeah.

Lenny beckons.

Aveling can wait.

Vince drove through Sandwich and up the A256 back the way he had come to Ramsgate. The rain was falling harder now, the roads were awash with roaring rivulets, and visibility was greatly reduced.

Ramsgate looked even greyer now than it did this morning. Much greyer.

Vince drove down Percy Street and around the block. No white Merc estates were in evidence. He dialled Tipper's number again on the mobile and got through to the answering machine once more.

Where was Tipper?

Fucking around in Margate in the aftermath of last night or what?

Vince parked up, donned his dark glasses again, just in case Tipper was about, and walked back to the basement flat. Nothing had changed down there. No sign of life. Just the curtains drawn and the rubbish bins and black bags rotting.

What to do?

It was tempting to break into the flat and turn it over. Who knows what you'd come up with? You'd have the jump on Tipper then.

But that was too risky. You're going to damage the door gaining access and he's going to notice *that* when he gets back...but he's going to enter the flat anyway, isn't he? Even if there is damage to the door, he's not going to hotfoot it down to the nick. No, like anyone else, he'd go inside and see what the rest of the damage is.

I'd be waiting for him, thought Vince.

Too risky?

What are the alternatives?

Park up and sit in the car and wait for the sucker to turn up? Phone him every so often to see when he's there just in case you miss him?

Mmmmm.

What'll it be?

In the meantime it'll be something to eat, thought Vince. Get myself something to eat.

The rain had abated so Vince walked up to the main drag and climbed the hill towards the centre of old Ramsgate. Somewhere along the High Street where it descends to the harbour he found a cheap fish-and-chips place, all Formica and strip lighting. That'll do nicely, said Vince to himself.

There was a young couple with two kids sitting in the window and nobody else. Vince went to the back of the place and ordered a large cod and chips and a cup of tea.

The food arrived in less time than it takes to say the word microwave and Vince wolfed it all down. He lingered over the cup of tea while looking through a *Daily Express* someone had left at an adjoining table. The bill came to £4.50 which Vince thought pretty reasonable.

Then he went for a stroll around Ramsgate harbour. Very picturesque. A lot of big private boats betokening a lot of money about down here.

He had a large vodka in a pub down at the front and then wandered back up the High Street. He stopped in a bookshop and checked through the paperbacks to see if there was anything worth reading. Acres of stuff on true crime and fictional crime, but none of that interested him.

Instead, he bought a volume of contemporary humorous quotations. It seemed amusing enough and didn't require too much concentration. The perfect book for whiling away an hour or two sitting in a car.

As Vince approached Percy Street he dialled up Tipper again. Still the answering machine.

Vince went around to the car and got in. It was a bit cold so he turned the ignition on and put the heater up. Then he had a snooze. For nearly an hour.

He came to in a sweat. The inside of the car was like a sauna. All the windows were closed and the heater was blasting away like a furnace in Hades. He turned off the ignition and stepped outside for some fresh air. The air was fresh all right, and very salty and very chill.

Now what to do?

Kill more time here waiting for Tipper to turn up? Or go back to Margate for an hour or two?

Let's try him again and then decide.

Vince pressed the REPEAT button on the mobile. The number showed up on the display and then began ringing.

Vince got back into the car.

'Yes?' said the voice on the phone.

The response was quick and caught Vince by surprise.

The voice then said, 'Hello?'

Then again after a couple of beats, 'Hello?' This time with irritation.

Vince continued listening and waiting.

'Is there anyone *there*?' The tone was now petulant and, perhaps, exasperated.

Then there was a long sigh and the phone was hung up.

Vince switched the mobile off and smiled to himself.

Lenny Tipper was going to have a big surprise and he was going to do a lot of talking. In fact he was going to talk until his fucking vocal cords packed up.

This guy was going to do more explaining in the next hour than he had done in the rest of his life.

And Tipper had no choice in the matter.

None whatsoever.

Vince got out of the car and locked it. He looked about. The streets were empty and silent.

Now's the time.

Vince walked across the road and on to the pavement opposite, his determined footsteps seemingly echoing in the damp night air.

The Walther's there all right thought Vince as he patted the shoulder holster. That's always good leverage in a situation like this.

What was this Lenny Tipper going to be able to tell him? How much did he know? How much of the big picture could he give him? Not all of it, that's for sure, because Vince had a nose for low-life like this guy, and his nose told him this asshole was pretty low on the totem pole. This guy was a monkey, not a grinder. He was carrying out orders, not giving them.

Still, I might be in for a surprise, thought Vince, he may know more than I think. Anyway, whatever he knows is more than I know. That's for sure.

Vince slowed his pace down as he drew closer to Tipper's basement. He looked up and down the street – nobody. He had the road to himself. There were going to be no witnesses to this little investigative exercise.

He stopped at the top of the steps that led down to the basement. The lights were on, but Vince couldn't see anything: the curtains, closed on what Vince presumed was the kitchen, and the whitewash on the inside of the front door saw to that. No passing strangers were going to gaze in on the world of Lenny Tipper.

Somewhere in there Mr T is going about his business, oblivious to his appointment with the Freedom of Information Act that had been formulated in Vince's head.

Vince hesitated. How was he going to play this? He hadn't thought that far ahead. What if Tipper doesn't answer the door? What if Tipper answers the door but it's on a security chain? What then?

He couldn't afford to give Tipper any time. He could do anything. He could get on the phone to whoever, he could vanish, he could...and Vince would be left high and dry. Tricky this.

Vince turned and hotfooted it back to the car. He unlocked the door, reached in and grabbed the small crowbar which he had earlier discovered in the boot (thanks, Larry!) and put it under his jacket. This would ensure there'd be no interruptions to the plan.

An old man was descending the main steps above Tipper's flat as Vince approached the house. Vince crossed the road and waited as the man took one slow and considered step at a time along the road and then round the corner and out of sight.

Vince walked back at a clip, glanced about, and then went down to Tipper's flat. The lights were still on inside and they partially lit the steps and the front. Vince sized up the front door. The paint was peeling and it appeared to be some cheap off-the-peg softwood door that had been in place for many years. There were two key locks on the left. One more than most people have, so security is high on Tipper's agenda. But the locks were somewhat voided by the glazing that constituted the upper half of the door. Still, entrance might not be that easy once you've smashed the glass if Tipper has deadlocks fitted. But it ain't going to be that hard.

Vince was impatient with himself.

Time to boogie.

There was no bell. Just a knocker above the letterbox.

Vince gave it a hefty bang. The dull metallic knock echoed.

Knock and wait.

One. Two. Three. Four. Five. Six. Seven. Eight. Nine. Ten. Nothing.

Knock again. Twice this time and harder.

Vince touched his shoulder holster for luck and lowered the crowbar that was clenched in his right hand.

A door opens or closes inside. There's a sound. Some footsteps. Footsteps approaching the front door. A cough. Then a voice, 'Hold *on*, Larry.'

That voice. Something nasty about the intonation, and something camp too.

Locks are being thrown inside the door, chains removed, bolts slid. The door starts to open and continues opening. Vince recognises Tipper as his shadower – the sunken eyes, the cadaverous appearance. Him all right.

Then that grating voice again, 'You're either early or late, *aren't* you?'

Tipper began this interrogative sentence with the expectation that Larry was standing on his doorstep, but by the time he got to the last two words and had raised his eyes he had realised it was Vince and, moreover, was imminently in receipt, full facially that is, of a fist.

Vince's fist connected with Tipper's face while his accelerating arm pushed open the door.

Tipper staggered back, put his hands to his face, let out a high-pitched scream and then crashed against a coatstand before falling to the floor.

Without taking his eye off Tipper Vince pushed the front door shut and secured a couple of bolts. Tipper was expecting someone and Vince didn't want them interrupting the little tête-à-tête he had planned.

The front door opened on to a corridor that led back into the basement. To the left, through an opened door, Vince could see the kitchen – dirty, grubby, 1950s cabinets, a gas cooker on legs, unwashed pots and crockery. The corridor had peeling wallpaper, a threadbare carpet, and a damp smell. Further down there were doors leading off it. Get Tipper down there and out of harm's way.

Tipper was lying on his back whimpering. He was holding his face and blood was pouring from his nose. It was then that Vince noticed his apparel, though perhaps apparel wasn't the right word. Costume might be better.

He was wearing black skin-tight leather trousers and a

matching jacket that was cut away to reveal his pierced nipples. He had studded leather belts and chains around his waist. On his feet was a pair of high-heeled boots. And a leather peaked cap was, surprisingly, still in place at a jaunty angle on his head, though whether the jaunty angle pre-dated the fist or not was a forensic point that was lost on Vince.

There was a smell about Tipper too. A smell that was now cutting through the damp odour of the basement. It was like some cheap heavy scent that took a lease in your nostrils. Sickly. Cloying. Muskish.

Vince grabbed Tipper by the collar and yanked him up from the floor and pushed him down the corridor. He was now sobbing.

'Down the end,' Vince hissed. 'Down the end, and don't make a sound.'

Tipper staggered along with Vince a few paces behind him holding the crowbar at waist height.

A door towards the end of the corridor was open. It appeared to be Tipper's bedroom if for no other reason than there was a bed in it on the far side. Brown linoleum, old and cracked, covered the entire floor area, and in the centre was a woolly crescent-shaped pink carpet like the ones you would expect to find in some old tart's premises in Soho. There was a heavy 1930s wardrobe with a door hanging off and a chest of drawers that had been painted white. The walls were bright green and punctuated with large posters. Gay posters. Young men with oiled bodies. Posing. Pouting. Provocative.

Vince shut the door behind them.

Tipper had staggered over to the bed and was lying on it, face down, still sobbing and still holding his face.

Approaching the bed Vince said, 'You know who I am, don't you? And you know why I'm here?'

There was a sniffled 'yes' from the leather-clad figure.

Vince continued, 'Now, you're going to start talking and you're going to come up with answers quicker than I can think of questions...got that?'

Tipper mumbled something.

Vince settled a hefty kick on Tipper just to get him in the mood.

But the reaction was not what Vince had expected.

Tipper spun round, screamed some frenzied cry and lunged with a horizontal slash at Vince, who was caught off guard. Tipper was holding a long, double-edged fighting knife and the top of the blade cut through Vince's trousers just below the right knee. It also cut through Vince's flesh to a depth of about a quarter of an inch.

Vince took several steps back in less time than it would take to think about doing it. He cursed himself for being caught unawares, cursed himself for not searching Tipper when he was down, and cursed himself for being such a sucker.

Tipper was off the bed now and coming towards Vince. His eyes were alight with homicidal intent.

Vince took a couple more steps back, the pain from the cut on his leg increasing with the passage of every second.

There was the knife thrusting at him, aiming for his chest. There was Tipper grinning at him like some demented Arabian assassin out for payback.

Vince had to get his head together, to relax. Plan his moves, take control of the situation. And he had to do it now.

The knife continued to thrust as Vince stepped back and moved around the room. Tipper was on a high, this was what he enjoyed doing. You could see it in his eyes. You could tell that this figured in his fantasies more than any of those oil-soaked young bodies on the walls who were the sole witnesses to this dangerous waltz.

Vince took a number of deep breaths and told himself he was relaxing. He relaxed his tense muscles, lowered his body temperature (or, rather, convinced himself he had), and distributed tranquillity throughout his mind.

Then he smiled at Tipper. Just a small, inconsequential little smile. Just enough of a smile to produce a reaction from this sadistic faggot.

'You're not going to have a face left to smile with. Know that, eh? You know that?' said Tipper in a mean, tremulous voice.

Vince knew a smile in a situation like this always disturbs the assailant. They can handle the violence, but they can't handle the smile.

Tipper lunged forward several times in quick succession. Vince took steps back and to the side each time. He had to ensure they kept to the open spaces of the middle of the room. If he ended up with his back to the wall it would be curtains for sure.

Another lunge forward by Tipper, this one perilously close to piercing Vince's chest.

Vince took a couple of extra steps back.

'You're not going to be about for much longer! Take in the sights because this is the last you'll ever see!' screamed Tipper.

'You better do a good job on me, old *fruit*,' replied Vince.

'I will,' said Tipper as he made a horizontal slashing movement. 'And when you're dead you're going straight to the incinerator! You won't even be dust, know that? Just *nothing*!'

Vince knew that while a weapon brought certain advantages to an assailant those advantages were actually outweighed by the disadvantages, particularly in the hands of an unskilled and undisciplined fighter. And whatever else Tipper was he wasn't anything more than a bar-room brawler. Vince knew this from the start.

The weapon is the focal point. Everything zeroes in on that weapon. It is the alpha and omega. Tipper's whole existence was now funnelling down to that blade. It was consuming him as, indeed, it would consume any similar street fighter. And, therefore, if it consumed all his attention and consciousness, there was little or nothing left for *thinking* about the fight.

Tipper was a single-goal automaton.

And this was something Vince was going to use to his

advantage. He couldn't have asked for better.

Tipper's thrusts at Vince's chest and stomach were becoming more frequent and less cautious.

Vince was still moving nimbly back and around but he knew that he did not have long. He had to move soon or he just might end up on the slab.

Vince tells himself to relax.

Vince smiles again at Tipper and knows that he now has to do it.

Tipper thrusts the knife forward at Vince's chest.

Now.

Vince doesn't move back as the knife approaches him. His feet remain stationary. He brings his arms round and forward with lightning speed as he simultaneously sinks down a few inches and thrusts back his groin and lower torso.

The thrusting knife prefixed to the right arm of Lenny Tipper continues speeding forward.

Lenny think he's on to a winner this time.

He really does.

Vince's arms continue to arc round in a pincer movement, the right arm drawing in to his own body while the left arm extends further out.

Then, with the knife only some six inches from his chest, Vince's right hand locks on to Tipper's wrist as his left hand, semi-opened and cupped, slams into Tipper's elbow. The sudden impact of these two hands moving in opposing directions with force on Tipper's arm produces a cracking sound.

Something snaps.

It is Tipper's arm.

Broken. Smashed.

A scream reverberates through the room. Then a whimper.

Vince slides his hand down Tipper's wrist to his hand and grasps the handle of the knife before slamming Tipper on the side of the head with his left arm and causing him to stumble forward and into the chest of drawers.

Then Vince is upon the supine Tipper and holding the tip of the knife firmly to the underside of his chin.

'OK, then. What's it going to be? Lights out or Answers 'R' Us?' asks Vince.

Tipper moans something. Vince isn't sure what he says.

'You know what?' continues Vince, 'I don't really care what you choose. I don't give a shit whether I get answers or total you. You know that? I'm easy. But I'm not patient.'

And on the word patient Vince pushed the knife forward so it just punctured Tipper's skin.

He let out another scream.

'Well, that's it. Say goodbye, Lenny. I've just run out of patience.'

'No! No! NO!!'

'Start filling me in then. From the top.'

Tipper continued to sob. Vince couldn't make out what he was saying. 'I'm running out of patience again. This is it. Say goodbye!'

'I'll tell you. Don't kill me!' implored Tipper.

'Talk!'

'You've broken my arm!'

'Talk!'

'Where do I begin? I mean, I don't know what to say.'

'Let's start at the beginning. You were following me. Why?'

'I had to keep an eye on you. See what you were doing. That's what they wanted me to do.'

'They, Tipper? They?'

'Yes. That's what they wanted.'

'Why?'

'I don't know. I really don't know. They were going to murder you like all the others. Because of your connection with Sid Blattner. I managed to put that together, but I don't know why. Believe me, I don't.'

'So you know about Harry? About Phil and Leo? About Lionel?'

'I've never murdered anyone. Never. Ever. I haven't been involved in anything like that. I just kept people under surveillance. That's all.'

'And then passed on information to people who did do the murdering. That's right, isn't it?' said Vince.

'But *I* didn't *murder* anyone.'

'But you were part of it. That makes you just as guilty! Just as fucking *guilty*!'

Tipper began sobbing again, complaining about his arm, and groaning. Vince really was running out of patience now. This slimeball didn't deserve to continue living.

Vince was angry. Answers weren't forthcoming. 'What do you know about Lionel's death?'

'Nothing. I read about it in the papers. That was before they got in touch with me.'

'Why did they get in touch with you?'

'I used to live in Bristol. I had a little private detective agency – civil, matrimonial, credit checks. Nothing heavy. Just small stuff like that. Then I got sent to prison. When I came out I couldn't go back there. Not back there to Bristol. So I moved down here. Ramsgate. About five years ago. Nobody knew me. I started up in business again. Clean slate, you know? When they contacted me they knew all about my time inside and I knew if I didn't go along with them they were going to let the story out and I'd be ruined down here. Everything I'd built up would come crashing down. Perhaps they knew someone I shared a cell with… something like that.'

'Carry on.'

'So I went along with it. And they paid me double my normal rate.'

Vince wanted to know what he was inside for?

Tipper was slow in answering so Vince prodded his chin again with the knife.

'I was inside for…*offences*.'

'Offences?'

'That's right.'

'What sort of fucking *offences*?'

'Sexual offences.'

'What was so special about yours then?'

Silence from Tipper.

Vince repeated himself. 'So what was so fucking special about your little offences?'

After a pause Tipper said quietly, 'Young people.'

Vince didn't want to know any more. 'Young people' could mean teenagers, could mean toddlers. He wouldn't put anything past Tipper.

Vince definitely didn't want to know. He didn't trust himself with this pile of shit. He could see himself terminating Tipper here and now, but he hadn't come for that. He was here to get information, find out what was going on. That's what he was doing. Nothing else.

'So how did they contact you?'

'They phoned me up. Then this guy comes round. Larry. He's Dutch. He's a butch blond in his early thirties. He's not the boss or anything. He's an intermediary. Passes messages. They want me to follow people up there in Margate. Report back to them. Nothing else.'

'Larry, eh?' said Vince. 'And he's who you were expecting tonight?'

'Yeah, he comes around and pays me. Cash. Always cash.'

'And you don't know anything more about him?'

'No, I don't. Honest.'

'Your curiosity never got piqued? You never followed him or anything?'

'No. I didn't want to know anything. I wanted to keep out of it. Just do my bit. Nothing else. No complications. Keep out of it all.'

The two biggest questions Vince had on this investigation were Why? and How? Why were Lionel and the others murdered? How did they know who was in Margate and when? Tipper obviously knew nothing about the Why? Beyond linking it in with Sid, but what about the How?

Vince held the knife tighter against Tipper's chin and

said, 'Start singing. How did they know who was arriving in Margate and where they were? Who told them or who told you?'

Tipper's eyes were full of fear as he stared up at Vince. 'Nobody. It wasn't difficult.'

Wasn't difficult? Nobody? *Wasn't* difficult!? How the fuck did they do it?

Tipper continued. 'They asked me to bug that old lady. Ma Spooner. I put a bug there. I put a few voice-activated bugs in her place. She lived alone. Didn't even have a canary. People turn up, they start talking, and the recording starts up.'

Christ, thought Vince. That simple. That fucking simple. It stared you in the face. Mrs Spooner was going to be the first port of call for anyone coming down from London and making inquiries. She knew Lionel better than anyone. She was with him virtually every day for thirty or however many years it was. She'd get a visit right away. Top of the list. See old Mrs Spooner. Which, of course, was what Phil and Leo did. Straight round to her place. We're here on behalf of Sid. We're staying round the corner at this hotel and you can contact us any time you like. Moths to the light. Spilling the beans. Setting themselves up as easy pickings. There you go. So simple it was dazzlingly elegant. Phil and Leo went straight there. And, indeed, so did I, thought Vince.

That's how they knew who had arrived and where they were staying.

Bugging Mrs Spooner.

But what about Aveling? Did he figure in this anywhere?

'You know a guy in Margate called Terry Aveling?'

Tipper shook his head. 'Never heard of him. Who is he?'

Vince took out his Walther. 'I'm only going to ask you this one more time. Do you know Terry Aveling?'

Tipper's eyes were filled with horror, he let out a shriek and said, 'No! No! I've never heard of him!'

Vince lowered the pistol and held it a few inches away from Tipper's forehead. 'Last time, Tipper.'

'I haven't. Honest! Never!'

Vince withdrew the pistol and re-holstered it. That clears that up. Aveling ain't in the loop.

'So you followed Phil and Leo when they arrived?'

'Yes. I did.'

'And sent reports back?'

'Yeah. I didn't know anything was going to happen to them. It was after. I see it in the papers, on TV. Larry said they had both been taken out.'

'What do you know about Harry?'

Tipper looked puzzled and angled his head like a dog. 'Who's Harry?'

'Sid's chauffeur, that's who.'

'Harry? Don't know anything about him. What's he got to do with it?'

'So you don't know anything about him?'

'Honest I don't.'

Vince believed him. It must have been soon after the funeral that Tipper was written into the proceedings. Whoever was the guiding hand behind this knew Sid wasn't going to start turning over the town and drawing attention to himself while the Old Bill were still thick on the ground and freshly enthusiastic in investigating Lionel's unfortunate demise.

'OK, so you don't know about Harry, but you know about me, don't you?' said Vince through his teeth.

Tipper nodded.

'So, you picked me up through the bug in Mrs Spooner's place and started trailing me. Right?'

'My arm's hurting badly,' whimpered Tipper.

Vince ignored his complaint and just said again, 'Right?'

Tipper nodded lamely. 'Yeah, and you were supposed to cop it in the hotel bedroom. But something went wrong. Then I was told to find out what had happened to you. Where you were...I need to get to the hospital. My *arm*.'

'All in good time, sunshine. I've got a few more questions for you. What do you know about Candy Green?'

'Little scrubber from Margate.'

'And?'

'Worked in a massage parlour there. Gave relief to Lionel once a week…and anyone else who had a few quid in notes to spare.'

'What part did she play in this?'

'She'd visited Lionel at home a couple of times. Borrowing money, I think. She went round there late at night. He opened the door and they were out of sight at the side. They grabbed him.'

'Then what?'

'I don't know. They killed him, didn't they? We all know that.'

'How come little Miss Green had such a strong alibi?'

'Larry said it was easy to put pressure on that Vicky woman who ran the place. They were up to a lot of no good. Had too much to hide. Giving Candy an alibi wasn't any sweat,' stated Tipper.

'Why did they take him, Lionel, to the dye works?'

'The dye works?' asked Tipper.

'Yeah. Where you followed me.'

'Oh, right. Round by the station. Right, yeah?'

'Uh-huh.'

'I don't know.'

'Why?'

'They had to take him somewhere. They couldn't off him outside Dreamland, could they? I don't know.'

Vince felt there was little point in asking this piece of shit any more questions. He'd coughed all he knew. It wasn't a lot, but it moved Vince on a few squares in this game.

What to do with Tipper?

Shoot him in the head and dump him out at sea? That would be the best solution but, unfortunately for Vince, that was not his style, much as he wished he could bring himself to do it.

What else?

Tie him up and just let him rot here?

Again, not Vince's style.

Tie him up, pro tem, make a getaway and then later tip off the Old Bill that they should investigate the basement?

Yeah. That would do perfectly. Tipper isn't going to 'fess who did this to him. He'd just be digging himself into deeper shit. There'd be too many questions. And, besides, the police would turn the place over and there'd be something here he shouldn't have and that would create more difficulties for him.

'You going to get me a doctor now?' implored Tipper.

'No. You'll have to wait a while, until I'm away.'

'What you going to do then?'

'Secure you for the present.'

Vince looked around the room. He didn't expect to find any cord or rope but there must be something, and there was – Tipper's collection of belts: hanging from a hook on the back of the door and sprawling in a mess on top of the chest of drawers. Vince riffled through them and found a couple of narrow ones made of pliant leather.

He returned to Tipper and knelt down. He secured his hands together behind his back and fastened his legs at the ankles. With his broken arm Tipper wasn't going anywhere at all.

'You just leaving me here?' asked Tipper plaintively.

'Somebody'll be along,' replied Vince as he exited through the door. 'Don't go away.'

Vince pulled the door shut firmly and looked up and down the corridor. He would have preferred to leave by the back door and through the gardens but, as he had discovered, there was no connecting alley and the prospect of scaling a dozen or so walls, aside from being physically exerting, guaranteed him being spotted by some law-abiding citizen out for a goodnight fag or calling the cat in. So, that wasn't really an option. He'd have to leave the way he came in. Through the front door.

The flat was silent now. The damp smell of the corridor reasserted itself.

Vince walked slowly and quietly down to the front door. He knelt and silently lifted the letterbox. All he could see were a few of the steps in front that ascended to the street and a little way either side of them. The scene was motionless and silent. No sign of anyone. No sign of Lenny's presumably poof friend either.

Vince let the letterbox flap fall back in place.

The whitewash on the inside of the front door's glazing prevented him from getting a better view so he went into the kitchen, leant over the sink that was full of rotting takeaway cartons and peered out through the end of the curtains. The view was narrow and restricted but showed that there was no one on the steps and no one loitering on the pavement above.

Vince returned to the front door and without making a sound turned the lock. He pulled open the door a few inches and looked out. All clear.

He opened the door fully, stepped out, and without turning, gently pulled it shut behind him. The night air was cold and had a musty, autumnal smell. Somewhere far off two cats were fighting.

Vince moved forward across the narrow space that separated the front door from the steps.

He was safe and would soon be out of here.

He'd go straight back to Margate, freshen up and give Marilyn a call. Perhaps she'd like to go out for dinner or something? Could be a really nice evening.

He placed his left foot on the first step and before he had a chance to raise his right foot something caught his attention. It was an indistinct movement to his left.

Indistinct and unexpected.

A movement out of nowhere.

Vince turned.

Something was heading towards him.

He had no time to react.

Whatever it was crashed into the side of his head.

It sent seismic waves careening through his mind.

He let out a gasp.

A liquid ran down the side of his head, over and under his shirt collar. It was warm and silky smooth and was issuing from somewhere above his ear.

Vince seemed frozen in time. One foot on the step. The radiating paroxysms of pain. The warm liquid.

The world around him began to shrink. It was like sitting on the back of a train that had just entered a tunnel. The circle of light got smaller and smaller.

And then it vanished.

And Vince's consciousness was extinguished.

9: Conclusion Riff

SID WAS SITTING at his desk in the back office at the club swearing, shaking, sweating, and staring at an array of small plastic tubs and bottles, each of which contained some pharmaceutical substance prescribed and provided by 'Dr' Flick, the 'Dr' now being purely a courtesy title since the good doctor had been struck off the Medical Register exactly a year ago to the day for embezzling funds from a wealthy woman patient with Alzheimer's Disease.

Flick had always looked after Sid and Sid wasn't going to let a disagreement with the British Medical Association prevent him from getting the level of treatment he had got used to and, indeed, in his eyes, deserved. The only difference now was that Flick had to instruct one of his cronies to write the prescriptions. Otherwise, it was business as usual in his consulting rooms in Harley Street.

But Flick wasn't coming up with the old magic this time. This olla podrida of nostrums, elixirs, potions, snake-oil and whatever-the-fuck just wasn't delivering.

Sid looked like shit.

And he felt like shit.

He hadn't shaved for four or five days, neither had he washed in that period or changed his clothes. And what sleep he had managed was fitful, light, and wrought with demons of anxiety that shot from the recesses of his mind whenever he closed his eyes.

Sid stared ahead at the tubs. One of them was to dissolve anxiety, one was to make him feel good, another was to counter the side effects of *that* one, and this other one *that* one, and somewhere one of them made him sleep. He was now in such a state that the prescribed regularity eluded him even though instructions were given on each tub. He was knocking back handfuls of tablets whenever he felt he needed them and washing them down with bourbon.

I'm ready for anything now, thought Sid, because I'm fucking invincible – totally, fucking *invincible*.

Sid was making a one-way descent into madness.

'We got Wally here, guv.'

Where did that voice come from?

Sid looked around the room. Nobody about.

Are they hiding or what?

'Guv, we got Wally here.'

The intercom, yes. It was Malcolm's voice on the intercom. Wally the journalist, yes. Sid felt better when he was talking to people. When he was *with* them. Sitting by myself ain't good for me, said Sid in a whisper to himself. Endless circles of black despair. Keep with people. Keep talking. Keep occupied. Keep doing things. Just got to get through this bad patch. I've got through worse. Yeah, lots of times. Have a bit of confidence in myself. Take charge. Get out there and do something. I'm Action Man, I am. Everybody tells me that.

Sid reached forward, cleared his throat, and pressed the intercom buzzer: 'Bring him in, Malcolm.'

'Coming, guv.'

The door opened as Sid was lighting a cheroot. Wally walked in followed by Malcolm.

Wally's usual effusiveness had deserted him. He looked grey and tired, world weary. He slumped down on the sofa and said, 'I wouldn't mind a drink, Sid.'

Sid ignored the request, got up from the desk and walked around to the sofa. He stopped about two feet in front of Wally, looked down at him, breathed cheroot smoke in his face and waited.

Wally said quietly, apologetically, 'I'm sorry, Sid, there's nothing to report.'

Sid smiled at Wally and then looked across to the grinning figure of Malcolm, all six feet five inches of him in his blue suit and floral tie and greased hair, and said, 'Malcolm, I think I must have misheard our old friend. It sounded like he said he had *nothing* to report. I couldn't have heard that right, could I?'

'Must have misheard it, guv. Ask him again,' replied Malcolm.

Sid looked down at Wally again, still smiling, still exhaling cheroot smoke and said, almost as a whisper, 'What have you got to tell us, old son?'

Wally looked up at Sid and then across at the grinning hulk and then back to Sid. His mouth opened but no sounds issued.

Sid took a step closer. 'What was that?'

Wally was on the verge of breaking down but he managed to say, 'There's nothing. Nobody knows anything down there. Aveling the copper has been burning the midnight oil trying to find out what's going on. Nobody knows *anything*.'

'Nobody knows anything!' screams Sid. 'How can nobody know *anything*. You tell me that!'

'They don't,' says Wally.

Sid continues screaming. 'I speak to Vince on Monday. Right? Speak to him then. Then he disappears. He doesn't contact me and I can't get hold of him. His mobile's off the air. And nobody knows *anything*? Now Thursday, ain't it?'

'Actually, it's Friday, Sid,' says Wally helpfully.

'Thursday! Friday! What's it matter? Vince has disappeared. He ain't contacted me since the beginning of the week and that spells just one thing to me. He's had it! They've got him! Vince is no longer in the land of the living. He's a corpse somewhere. Right? And you come here and tell me that nobody knows *anything*!'

'I'm afraid so, old man,' replies Wally.

'What else you found out about this Tipper geezer then, *old man*?' spits Sid.

'Well, like I told you. He has this paedophile record down in Bristol and then he moved to Ramsgate and ran this detective agency. But he kept his nose clean and the local police have never had any complaints about him, so Terry Aveling says. He's disappeared too. Nobody knows where he is.

'But Sid, you must remember, no offence has been committed down there. The police aren't involved. This is just Terry nosing about himself. I mean you could go along to the police in Thanet and tell them about Vince and say you suspect foul play and they'll start nosing about and, you know, the whole can of worms —'

'You think I'm a cunt, Wally? Eh? You think I'm a total and utter cunt, eh? You think I'm going along to the police and making a complaint?'

'No, Sid, I was talking hypothetically.'

'You think I'm a cunt, don't you?'

'No, Sid, honestly. I was merely talking hypothetically. That's all.'

'I'll tell you what's going to happen. I'm going down there myself and sort this out once and for all, because no other fucker I send down there seems to have the bottle and the wherewithal to do it for me. You know that? Even turns out Vince is a tosser and can't cut it. I should have known it. If I ever want a job done right I have to do it myself. A simple lesson I should have learnt a long time ago. Know that?'

Wally pushes himself up from the sofa and says, 'That really isn't prudent, Sid. You going down there yourself. It's a trap down there. They're just waiting for you to walk into it.'

Sid turns in a rage and grabs Wally by the lapels and shouts in his face, 'You saying I can't handle myself? Eh? That what you're saying? Eh? You *do* think I'm a cunt, don't you? You think I can't go down there and get this sorted?'

Wally shakes his head. 'I'm not saying that. I'm not. Really I'm not, Sid. It's safer for you staying here. Don't risk it.'

Sid pushes Wally forcefully back on to the sofa and then stands over him and says in quiet, measured tones, 'I told you, didn't I, that if you didn't come up with anything it was going to be a one-way trip to the Essex marshes? You remember me saying that?'

Wally nods in agreement.

'Well, I *was* going to demonstrate a bit of the leniency for which I'm noted, but when you start telling me I'm a cunt, I find I've just run out of leniency. Know that? You, old son, are off to the estuarine salt marshes.'

Sid looks across to Malcolm and points to Wally who is now crying and begging Sid to forgive him. Malcolm, still with a grin from ear to ear, pulls Wally up off the sofa and pushes him out of the room.

Sids says to himself, 'I should have got that piss-artist taken out there years ago.'

Malcolm drove off telling Wally that dumping bodies in the marshes 'out east' was one of *his* favourite hobbies but, in fact, that was not where he dumped Wally. He dumped him outside El Vino's in Fleet Street, figuring that Sid could not really have meant what he said, thereby demonstrating again, beyond any doubt, that he could not divine Sidney Blattner's true intentions under any circumstances.

Wally went straight into the bar and it took him two bottles of Château Margaux to sober up. And, uncharacteristically, he had not a word to say about what had befallen him (though, many years later, in a volume of memoirs, *Crime on My Patch*, an entirely self-serving fictionalised account did appear that accused Sid of kidnapping him).

Meanwhile Sid had been relaxing in his office watching porno video films. He didn't like modern pornos that were shot in colour with beautiful girls with hair-dos and lip gloss and with synch sound and music, no. He liked those mute black-and-white films that were made in London in the 1960s. The ones shot in some dingy bedsit in Earls Court or wherever.

Those were the type Sid liked.

He sat there on the sofa eating several Big Macs and drinking Sainsbury's Diet Classic Coke while running the tapes and laughing nervously to himself. Then he fell asleep with mayonnaise dribbling down his jacket.

Malcolm returned shortly after 1 p.m. and woke Sid up. Sid didn't ask about Wally and Malcolm didn't volunteer any information. The soak of a journalist was no longer in the picture in Sid's mind, he was being translated into methane gas somewhere the other side of Southend-on-Sea.

Malcolm asked Sid how he was?

Sid just sat on the sofa staring ahead. Catatonic.

Malcolm asked if he needed anything?

Sid then stood bolt upright, still staring ahead.

Malcolm wasn't sure what to do.

Sid remained motionless, breathing heavily and rapidly.

Should Malcolm get a doctor or what? He didn't know.

Sid did not move. His eyes were wide open and un-blinking, still staring ahead. There was an eeriness about him that unsettled Malcolm. It was as though Sid was possessed. As though he was going through a metamorphosis. And, indeed, he was. Sid's mind was cranking up into ever higher gears.

Malcolm left the room to see if the two Daves had arrived and to make a couple of phone calls and to get a sandwich and coffee. When he returned about half an hour later Sid was sitting behind his desk going through some papers. He looked up, smiled and said, matter of factly, in what Malcolm took to be his normal voice, 'Are we all ready?'

Malcolm was puzzled by the sudden change in Sid. He no longer appeared to be racked with anxiety, fear and anger. His face was as calm as his manner.

Not getting a response forced Sid to repeat himself.

'Malcolm? Are we all ready?' He said this patiently.

'Yes, guv. We're ready,' answered Malcolm. 'The two Daves are here. They'll travel down with us in the Merc. And Les will be making his own way there in the Transit. That'll be handy if we need to do any visiting and want to keep it low profile.'

'Good. And everyone is tooled up?'

'Up to the eyeballs, guv. And rarin' to go. The best team of heavies that could be put together at short notice.'

Sid nodded and smiled again and then looked at his watch. 'It's 2 p.m. now. I've got a couple of things to do and I need to take a shower. We'll leave at about 3.30? How about that?'

'It's a Friday, guv. Traffic is horrendous.'

'*I* never seem to have any problem with traffic, Malcolm.'

'You say so, guv.'

'Right, then.'

Sid made a few phone calls to accountants and lawyers and then went upstairs to his apartment where he shaved, showered and changed his clothes. He made himself a cup of coffee and some toast and skimmed through *The Times*. Then he returned to the office. He phoned Miriam and told her that he would be going away for a couple of days. She

didn't seem remotely interested. Then he dealt with the
mail that had been sitting on his desk since 9 a.m. There
were several circulars, a couple of lawyer's letters, state-
ments from four different banks, something from the local
council regarding health and safety standards and, lastly, a
buff-coloured Jiffy bag.

This was the video.

Sid's name and the address of the gambling club off
Curzon Street had been written in green felt tip pen, all in
caps, inexpertly on the front.

It had been posted first class.

An innocent Jiffy bag.

There was no return address though there was a postmark.

The postmark should have warned Sid.

But he didn't look at it.

It said MARGATE.

The date was yesterday.

Sid opened the package and took out an unmarked, black
video cassette. There was a square purple Post-It note
stuck to it and handwritten on that, in the same felt pen as
the Jiffy bag, was the statement: *Sid – You'll enjoy this.*

Sid knew what it was right away. Or, rather, he thought
he knew what it was: that slag down in St George's Square
was going to make a lesbian video with her girlfriend. Sid
had given her a camcorder and told her exactly what he
wanted to see. He had a fondness for porno films with
girls he knew. A real fondness.

Barbara was willing to do everything he asked, including water sports and fist-fucking.

Sid looked at his watch and decided that he could afford
ten minutes or so to get a taster of it.

He put the cassette in the player, went over to the sofa,
pressed the required buttons on the remote, lit up a cheroot
and sat back to enjoy some Sapphic high jinks, or so he
thought. In fact, he was about to discover just why Lionel
was taken out to the dye works.

The screen was black. Then it flickered. There was white interference and then the hiss of ambient sound.

A figure appeared standing in the centre of the frame. It was Lionel. His hands were tied in front of him. He was standing in a factory of some kind, certainly an industrial premises.

Just standing there.

Looking straight into the camera.

Waiting for something.

A muffled and indiscernible voice says something off screen. Lionel looks to his left and listens and then nods his head and looks into the camera again. He says, 'Sid, I'm all right...I think they're going to ask you for ransom money... they are.'

Lionel continues staring straight ahead and then, suddenly, a figure appears from frame left and moves towards Lionel. The figure holds up something. A small gun. There's a bang that overloads the sound level and a momentary flash.

Lionel has been shot in the head. Blood spurts out of the wound as he falls back.

Then the screen is black.

Dave 1 was driving and Dave 2 was sitting in the front passenger seat. Malcolm was in the back of the Merc with Sid who was carefully filing his fingernails.

The traffic had been heavy and slow all the way down to Bromley but now the road was clear and Dave 1 was giving it plenty of welly on the M2 somewhere south-east of Rochester.

Malcolm turned and looked out the back window. He couldn't see what he was looking for so he swung himself around again and said to Dave 1, 'You've lost Les.'

'Yeah,' replied Dave 1, 'stands to reason. We got six litres and he's only got two...and they're diesel.'

'He'll get lonely,' observed Dave 2.

Sid said, 'We'll see him at the hotel later.'

'Right, guv,' agreed Malcolm.

The next five or so miles were passed in silence and then Sid said, 'I got a video in the post today.'

'Oh, yeah. Some good action, eh, Sid? Anyone we know?' said Dave 1.

'Wasn't that type of video at all. Whoever's behind all of this sent me a video of Lionel being shot in the head. Right in the head. Point blank,' said Sid in a disturbingly cheery voice.

Nobody knew what to say. There was an ominous silence.

Sid continued, 'This geezer goes up to Lionel and it's BANG! Straight in the head. You can see it all.'

Malcolm and the two Daves remained silent. They were all speechless.

Sid continued in his breezy manner. 'Course, it'll take more than *that* to unsettle me. If they think some little video's going to put me off my stroke they'll have to think again. Won't they, eh?'

Sid chuckled to himself and returned to filing his nails.

Malcolm felt an icy shiver run down his back. He began to think that he'd sooner be somewhere else.

The two Daves exchanged glances. They each knew what the other was thinking, but neither of them could guess what Sid was thinking save to say, whatever it was, it was now beyond the realms of mere sanity.

The remainder of the journey passed in silence except for Dave 1 asking somewhere east of Canterbury whether anyone wanted to take a slash? There had been no reply. Sid had continued doing his nails in some obsessive ritual and humming to himself. The journey couldn't end soon enough for the other three.

Dave 1 pulled into the forecourt of the Imperial Towers hotel just before 7 p.m.

Sid pressed the button that electrically lowered the window in the back of the Merc and looked out. 'What sort of poxy fucking hotel is this then?'

Malcolm coughed and said, 'It's the biggest hotel in Margate, Sid. The only one that could do what we want.'

Sid scowled. 'Looks like a bleedin' mum-and-dad bed-and-breakfast shit heap to me!'

'Yeah,' chipped in Dave 2, 'this is the best they can do down here. Anyway, beautiful views over the sea, they say.'

'Wouldn't put my dog in a place like this,' concluded Sid who had never owned a dog in his life.

The hotel was on the cliffs just up the road from where Vince had stayed in the Trade Winds, about five minutes' walk, if that.

They checked in and the two Daves carried Sid's luggage up to his suite on the third floor that overlooked the sea. The single rooms either side of the suite were reserved for the Daves while Malcolm and Les shared the double room directly opposite.

Sid's suite consisted of a large bedroom with bathroom and a lounge with a sofa, armchairs and television.

'Now, listen carefully,' said Sid as he sank down in the sofa, 'and I'll tell you what's what. I'll be sleeping in *there* and I want one of you in *this* lounge throughout the night *and* tooled up. Right? I don't care how you sort it amongst yourselves as long as there's someone right here all night. Understand?'

There were three nods.

'Any questions?' asked Sid.

'You suppose Les has got lost?' asked Malcolm.

'I just spoke to him on his mobile,' said Dave 2, 'he's only up the road. Be here in twenty minutes or so.'

'Thank Christ for that,' sighed Malcolm. 'I thought we might have lost someone already.'

Sid leapt from the sofa and ran at Malcolm, pushing him into the drinks bar. 'Don't you ever make jokes like that! Hear me?'

'Sorry, Sid. I really didn't mean anything,' said Malcolm apologetically as he got up from the carpet.

'Don't you ever!' hissed Sid. 'Ever!'

The two Daves exchanged glances again.

'Right,' said Malcolm changing the subject, 'what are our plans then, Sid?'

Sid returned to the sofa and gave the question some thought. 'We'll have a nice meal downstairs and then an early night. Tomorrow we'll see the copper, but first we're going over Ramsgate way to see about this geezer named Tipper. We'll go in the Transit for that. Saturday morning, most of the folks will be out shopping and doing their business, so it should be a bit peaceful there.'

Dave said, 'What if he's not in, Sid?'

'In that case we let ourselves in, make ourselves at home and wait for him,' said Sid who felt he was only stating the obvious.

'What time should we leave?' asked Malcolm.

'I'd say nine o'clock sharp. OK?'

The three of them murmured agreement with Sid who then added, 'If nobody else can find Tipper, perhaps we can, eh? Finding him is the key to unlocking this little mystery...and we're a pretty resourceful bunch of faces, aren't we?'

The following morning, a few minutes after 9 a.m., Sid walked out of the front of the hotel following Malcolm and flanked by the two Daves. They walked in silence along Fort Crescent and down a small side road to where Les was waiting for them with the windowless Transit.

'Morning, Sid,' said Les.

'Morning,' replied Sid. 'Let Malcolm have the keys to this and he'll give you the keys to the Merc. Bring it back here and follow us at a distance. If the shit hits the fan I want you up in the rear ready to speed us away. Right?'

'No worries, guv. None at all.'

'And one other thing, Les. This ain't traceable, is it? This Transit?' asked Sid.

'No. It was nicked over Harringay way on Thursday night. And I put new plates on it,' said Les reassuringly.

Sid nodded. He was well pleased.

Les walked off to fetch the Merc while Malcolm unlocked the Transit and they all climbed in.

'You do the driving, Malcolm,' stated Sid.

Malcolm nodded.

Dave 1 sat in the front with Malcolm while Dave 2 joined Sid in the back on the bench seat that Les had especially fitted on Friday morning for the jaunt.

Sid took out his notebook and found a page that said in green Biro:

> *Leonard Henry Tipper*
> *Basement Flat*
> *33 Percy Street*
> *Ramsgate*

Sid unfolded a street map of Thanet and searched the index for Percy Street. He soon found it and then threw the map, unfolded, over his shoulder.

'Les is up front, guv,' said Malcolm.

'OK. I'll direct you. Straight down here and take a left along the front and we'll get on the Ramsgate road.'

'Got you.'

'By the way, Malcolm,' said Sid, 'you got any reply on Tipper's number yet?'

'No, I told you, Sid. It's been disconnected.'

'So you did. Well, if we find chummy himself we can disconnect him too, eh? One limb at a time. That would make him holler! Huh! Yeah, I'd do that myself!' said Sid in a gloatingly sick voice.

This sojourn couldn't be over quick enough for Malcolm and the two Daves now. They were all thinking the same thing: get this over with, get back to London, and start putting some distance between us and Sid. He's going around the bend for sure, but he can fucking well do *that* by himself. He ain't going to take us with him.

Malcolm continued along the Margate seafront until Sid

told him to take a left down Belgrave Road. Les followed them at a comfortable distance. Then it was down Eaton Road and soon Margate had been left behind as they headed south to Ramsgate.

Sid took out his 9mm semi-auto and slipped a magazine in. He chambered a round and then took a couple of other mags from his shoulder bag and stuffed them in his jacket pocket. 'Rest of you guys got your shooters at the ready? Just in case?'

'Yes, guv,' said Malcolm.

Dave 1 turned from the front seat, patted his shoulder and confided, 'She's primed and ready.'

Dave 2 unholstered his Smith & Wesson .45 Magnum revolver and spun the chambers. 'You lot go with sissies' pistols. This is the real thing, *girls*.'

Dave 1 and Malcolm laughed but Sid didn't find it funny. 'You just make sure you know how to use it. That's all I ask. And no jokes. Right? Didn't I say that already?'

Dave 2 re-holstered the firearm after momentarily toying with the idea of concluding this whole operation right now by giving it to Sid between the eyes.

'That's the Ramsgate viaduct up ahead,' said Sid a few minutes later.

'So?' said Malcolm.

'The turning we want is up on the left somewhere. A few turnings up. Up the hill. Percy Street.'

Malcolm dropped down into third while he and Dave 1 kept a vigilant eye out, and there it was – Percy Street. Malcolm pulled over and stopped the vehicle and inquired, 'What do you want to do now, guv?'

Sid caressed his gun as he thought for a moment and then said, 'Turn down the street and have a slow drive by. We'll see what we can see.'

'Right,' said Malcolm as he pulled forward.

He took the left and headed down Percy Street.

'What number is it, Sid?' asked Dave 1.

'Thirty-three. Number 33.'

'Uh-huh. That's this side. Up ahead a bit further,' said Dave 1.

Sid told Malcolm that he was driving too slow, to speed it up otherwise they'd attract attention to themselves.

'There it is,' said Dave 1, 'just there.'

Sid stood forward and looked out the window over Dave 1's shoulder. 'Looks a right dump to me.'

'Does a bit,' said Malcolm.

'Right, continue down here and around the block,' Sid ordered.

'If we come back down the road again we can park up almost opposite the place. There are a few spaces there,' suggested Dave 1.

'Yeah, do that,' said Sid to Malcolm.

'Right, guv.'

Sid dialled Les up on the mobile. 'Les?'

'Yes, guv?'

'We're going round the block. Follow us. We'll be parking on the street we've just come down, on the right.'

'Uh-huh.'

'You park up behind us, towards the main road and *facing* the main road. Understand?'

'Understand, yeah.'

'Just in case.'

'Just in case, yes.'

'And one other thing, Les.'

'What's that, guv?'

'Keep the engine running.'

'I'll do that.'

Sid pressed the button on the mobile and concluded the call.

'Nearly there, Sid,' said Dave 1.

Malcolm pulled the Transit over to the right and parked behind a Citroën 2CV. He turned the engine off and said, 'There's his place. Over there on the left.'

Sid took a pair of binoculars out of his bag and pointed them at No. 33. 'Fucked if I can see anything. Just a grubby old tenement. Fuck all going on there, son.'

'Les is parked up now, guv. Just back there,' said Dave 1.

'On the other side?' asked Sid.

'Yeah.'

Sid climbed over the seat and went to the back of the van. He peered out through a gap in the improvised curtains Les had gaffer-taped up on Friday. He could see the Merc up there on the right, some forty yards or so shy of the Ramsgate Road. Good. He was in place.

'What's the best way to handle this now?' Malcolm inquired.

'The best way,' Dave 2 volunteered, 'is for me and Dave to hop over there and have a nose about. If he's not in we'll force the door and have a sniff about.'

'That sounds good,' said Sid. 'You two got all you need?'

'We got more than we need,' added Dave 1.

'Let's do it then,' said Dave 2.

Dave 1 opened the door and got out. Dave 2 climbed over the passenger seat and joined him. They looked like a couple of lads in the building trade as they trucked casually across the street.

Malcolm climbed back to the bench with Sid and pulled the curtains across that Les had rigged up behind the front seats.

'Don't close them. We won't be able to see what's going on,' protested Sid.

'I'll leave a gap. It's just that people might think it a bit odd. Two guys, you know, just sitting in the back here,' said Malcolm.

He left a gap and he and Sid sat forward following the progress of the two Daves as they arrived at Tipper's flat. They stopped on the pavement by the steps that led down to the basement and Dave 1 produced a pack of cigarettes and took out one. He offered the pack to Dave 2 who also took out one.

'What they doing stopping for a fucking fag!' hissed Sid.

Malcolm replied, 'That's just to cover them while they

give the basement the old once over and see that's it's all clear.'

'You don't say,' replied Sid sarcastically.

The two Daves light their cigarettes and puff and chat away and then, casually, they step off the pavement and descend the steps. All perfectly normal like.

'It's 9.25 a.m.,' says Sid looking at his gold Rolex. 'Shouldn't take them long, should it?'

'Depends what they find,' says Malcolm.

Sid climbed over the seat and peered out the back curtain. 'Les is still there. Hope he's checked the petrol...just in case.'

Malcolm said, 'No worries, guv. Dave tanked it up this morning.'

'I'm glad we've got something right. Very glad indeed,' observed Sid sourly as he returned to the seat. Then, 'I don't suppose we got a daily paper here, have we?'

'No.'

Sid grunted with displeasure and then reached back for the map of Thanet which he began studying closely. He also started humming and this disturbed Malcolm.

Malcolm was keeping his eyes on No. 33, Percy Street. He was sprung and ready for action should anything happen.

Sid continued humming. A loud, unmelodic humming that filled the inside of the Transit. Malcolm tried to block it from his mind but found it impossible.

Then Sid said, 'You know, looking at this map, all these names and that, it's *my* history here.'

Malcolm wasn't sure what to make of the statement and just murmured, 'Oh, really, Sid?'

'Yeah. My *history*. All these names mean so much... to me...I know what they all *mean*...to me.'

Malcolm nodded and continued staring through the gap in the curtains over to No. 33. Sid resumed the humming.

Minute followed minute with seemingly decreasing rapidity. Malcolm was getting concerned about the passage of time, about the non-reappearance of the two Daves. He couldn't understand it.

Something was wrong.

Something was definitely wrong.

Malcolm stole a glance out of the corner of his eye. Sid was still poring over the map, still humming. And seemingly unconcerned over the passage of time.

They're two dependable guys, the two Daves. They know how to look after themselves. They know what they're doing, they do. Yeah. Nothing to worry about on that score. They always come up trumps. Too fly to be caught out, they are. They've been in some pretty hairy situations. Always know how to come out on top.

Nothing could beat them. They're the best.

Any minute now they'll be out. Smiles across their faces. With the full story. No doubt about that. Any minute now. You just wait and see.

Any minute.

The two of them.

That's right.

Malcolm's attempts at cheering himself up and putting a good gloss on the situation were getting more difficult by the second.

Something was wrong.

They'd be back by now, surely?

Malcolm slyly pushed back the sleeve of his bomber jacket. He didn't want Sid to notice he was checking his watch. He looked down at the digital face without moving his head and saw the time: 9.50 a.m.

Twenty-five minutes down there?

Twenty-five!

What the fuck were they doing?

Cooking themselves a big fry-up breakfast and doing a spot of gardening?

Twenty-five fucking minutes!

No two ways.

Something was wrong.

Very wrong.

Malcolm turned to Sid and said as coolly as he could manage, 'Sid, we've got a problem here.'

Sid stopped humming and then slowly lifted his eyes from the map. '*We've* got a problem?'

'Yeah, a problem. It's nearly half an hour now.'

'Malcolm, old son,' said Sid in a silky smooth psychotic voice, '*I* do not have problems. *You* certainly have one, but I do not.'

Before Malcolm could decipher what he was being told Sid had produced his 9mm pistol and was holding it to his head. 'Now, Malcolm, sort *your* problem out. Get over there and find out what's going on, otherwise I'll shoot your head off here and now. You're expendable. I'm not. Got me?'

'Come on, Sid, this is no time for joking about.'

'Who's joking? I'm deadly serious, son. You get over there and down those steps and sort this out or else you're going to be snuffed right now.'

There was a maniacal look in Sid's eyes. There were beads of sweat arrayed along his forehead and upper lip. There was an odour of insanity about him. Malcolm could smell it. It was thick and heavy in the air.

'Right, Sid. But let's just give it a few more minutes. I'm sure they'll be up any time now.'

Sid spoke slowly and coldly. 'You can either go *now* to the basement or you can go *now* to meet your maker. The choice is yours. Me? I don't give a tuppenny what you choose. Savvy, eh? *Savvy?*'

Sid prodded Malcolm in the side of the head with the muzzle of the pistol. Malcolm pulled away and said, 'Right, Sid. Right, I'm going.'

He had to get out of the van and away from this madman. Anything was better than staying here, cooped up with this insanity.

'Don't try anything on, Malcolm. I'll be covering you with the shooter from here to the basement. One wrong move and you'll have it in the back. And you know what a good shot I am, don't you?'

Malcolm nodded.

Sid then took Malcolm's pistol out of his shoulder holster.

'Sid, you can't expect me to go over there unprotected, can you?'

'Yes I can. And another thing. If you try and cross me on this I'm phoning Silas and he'll go round and take care of your wife and little daughter. Got that?'

Malcolm nodded again.

'Now get over there and get the full story.'

Malcolm parted the curtains, climbed over the front seat and let himself out. Sid sat down in the front and pulled the door shut, then he wound the window down and said, while pointing the 9mm at Malcolm, '*This* is following your every move, son. And it ain't got a conscience.'

Malcolm looked down the barrel of the semi-automatic and then raised his eyes. Sid was grinning at him. A full facial insane grin. And glowing eyes. Asylum eyes.

This here is the devil, thought Malcolm, and that over there is the deep blue sea.

He wondered how it was that he now found himself in this situation? What mysterious, occult conjunctions in his life had conspired to get him here?

Here.

Now.

He knew the answers, of course, but what use were they? How could they improve the present circumstances of his life? They couldn't.

Only one thing to do.

Turn and start walking.

'What you waiting for then?' said Sid as he poked the pistol in Malcolm's direction. 'Get *moving*!'

'Just going, Sid.'

Malcolm turned, looked up and down the street, and crossed diagonally towards No. 33. The first steps were the most difficult and then an adrenalin high kicked in and

Malcolm found a springiness in his step. He'd confront whatever was down there in the basement and he'd deal with Sid as well. Sid had overstepped the mark. This was well out of order.

Up on to the pavement now, a couple more steps and here are the railings and there is the flat down there.

The door to the basement was slightly ajar. Malcolm could see the splintered wood of the frame where the two Daves had forced their entry with a crowbar. Mute testimony indeed to their presence.

There were no sounds coming up from the basement.

Malcolm looked over his shoulder back to the Transit. He could see Sid sitting in the front seat staring in his direction, holding the pistol under the map that had fascinated him so.

No choice here, mate, Malcolm said to himself. Down you go.

One step.

Two steps.

Three steps.

Four steps.

Five steps.

So far so good.

And then a few more steps and Malcolm was at the bottom. He stopped and waited and listened.

He went to the front door and slowly pushed it open a few inches. Then a few inches more.

Silence.

He opened the door further and looked down a long corridor. There was no movement. No sign of life.

Malcolm stepped into the flat and waited again. He was shaking somewhat and his body felt both cold and clammy. His own breathing seemed to echo around his head.

He looked to the left and saw the kitchen. The dirty, greasy kitchen. Above the cooker was a rack of knives that included a large carving knife. Better to have some sort of weapon than no weapon at all, Malcolm told himself.

He looked down the corridor again. Nothing had changed. But now he noticed the insinuating musty smell of damp that seemed to hang there like a fog.

Malcolm took several quick steps into the kitchen and removed the large knife from the rack. He ran his thumb lightly down the blade. It wasn't that sharp, but it was sharp enough and, besides, the tip was the business end anyway.

He now worked his way down the corridor. The first door on the left was open half way. He could see a dining-room table and some chairs and a sideboard. He unclipped the Mag-Lite from his belt and shone the torch around. Nothing.

The door on the opposite side opened on to a WC. Nothing there apart from a poster of some drag artiste on the wall.

Malcolm crossed to the next door up on the other side. It was closed. He opened it. It was a store room: an exercise machine, a bicycle, old books and magazines and packing chests. And a very damp smell.

The bathroom on the other side was empty. The lino on the floor was rotting. Nobody had ever cleaned the place.

He now paused again and listened.

Silence.

Except for the wind whistling down a flue somewhere.

There was nobody here. Malcolm was sure of that. The place was deserted.

But he couldn't take chances.

He crossed the corridor again and gently pushed open another door. It was a bedroom. The light was on. An un-made bed, a chest of drawers, a wardrobe, gay posters on the wall and not much else.

The other rooms were also empty: another bedroom, this one smaller, a box room really, and a further store room that appeared to have been converted into a dungeon with 'blocks of stone' wallpaper, manacles fitted high up on the wall, an old dentist's chair with leather straps and all the usual paraphernalia of the pain-and-pleasure crowd.

Malcolm peered round and looked up and down the corridor from the dungeon. There was still no sound or movement. Malcolm thought it likely that if anything was going to happen to him it would have happened by now.

But you can't be sure.

Especially in a situation like this.

You can't be *sure*.

There was one door left. The door at the end of the corridor. It was a glass door with a wooden frame painted green, only you couldn't see in as curtains were hung on the other side of it. One of those doors.

Malcolm continued looking at it from the dungeon. If anything is finally going to happen....

The green door.

What lies behind the green door?

Malcolm took a couple of steps towards it, stopped and waited. Nothing.

A couple more steps. Wait and listen.

Three more and Malcolm was touching the door.

He waited again.

He put his ear to the jamb, closed his eyes and strained to hear something, anything.

There was nothing.

Silently Malcolm put the Mag-Lite back in his belt clip, grasped the carving knife tightly in his right hand and raised it to chest height.

He placed his left hand on the door handle and counted down....

Ten.

Nine.

Eight.

Seven.

Six.

Five.

Four.

Three.

Two.

One.

Now.

Malcolm's hand pushed down on the handle. There was a loud metallic click that he ignored, figuring he was now in too deep to worry about any sound he might make. His damp hand continued down until it could go no further. He pushed the door open a few inches and stopped.

There were no gunshots.

There were no voices saying 'Come in, we've been expecting you' or 'Don't try anything. We've got you covered.' None of that.

None of anything.

Just silence.

Malcolm resumed pushing the door open until he could see what was beyond this, the green door.

It was a lounge that opened on to the garden with French windows occupying the whole length of the far wall. There were old but still brightly patterned drapes at either end. The walled garden beyond was seriously over-grown. A bird started singing in an elder tree.

Malcolm took a step into the room. There were bean bags scattered about, a deep-pile pink circular carpet by a coffee table, more gay posters on the wall, a sound system and two speakers on a trestle table covered with grey felt, a two-drawer filing cabinet with file folders stacked on top of it.

Malcolm pushed the door back further so he could see the other half of the room.

There was a leather sofa —

Dave 2 was on the sofa. On his back, his eyes wide open, staring up at the ceiling. The side of his head was matted blood. He was long dead.

On the floor in front of the sofa was Dave 1 face down in a sea of blood. Nothing much remained of the back of his head. Someone had bludgeoned him into the after-life.

Malcolm looked quickly around the room again just to

make sure there was nothing else. One of the French windows was ajar. Whoever had done this had made their escape through the garden.

And it was time Malcolm made his escape – if you call scurrying back to Sid Blattner an escape.

Malcolm put the carving knife under his jacket and stepped back into the corridor. The sooner he was out of here the better.

He walked quickly down the corridor, through the front door and up the steps. There was nobody about on the street aside from small kids playing some game at the end of the terrace.

Malcolm stepped out and headed for the Transit van. Sid must have climbed over into the back again as his menacing figure was no longer to be seen in the front passenger seat clutching the 9mm pistol.

Sid ain't going to take this news too well, thought Malcolm. He'll go ballistic. Still, if I have to, thought Malcolm, I'll knife him before he has a chance to do anything. I've levelled the playing field a little.

When Malcolm got to the Transit he saw the front passenger door wasn't quite shut. He remembered Sid slamming it shut when he sent him out. Had Sid stepped out for some fresh air or what?

Malcolm pulled the door open and said, 'Sid?'

He climbed in and pushed back the curtains. There was the bench seat but there was no Sid. The van was empty.

Malcolm jumped out and looked up and down the street. There was no Sid to be seen.

Perhaps Les knows where he is?

He ran down the street and then suddenly stopped. The Mercedes had gone.

No Sid. No Les. No Merc.

Malcolm ran back to the other end of the street hoping to see or find something – he didn't know what but he thought there might be something.

But there wasn't.

He walked back to the van and climbed in.

Yes, indeed. The keys were still in the ignition. He turned it and the diesel engine started up.

I'm out of here and gone, Malcolm told himself. Out of this completely. Finito.

He swung the Transit out, did a U-turn in Percy Street and was soon heading up the Ramsgate Road. Next stop London.

Malcolm thanked the gods for smiling on him today. That's the least he could do for them.

But Sid?

What had happened to Sid?

Sid?

Come to think of it, Malcolm didn't give a fuck about what had happened to Sid.

Not a fuck.

And Malcolm would never know what a big favour Sid did him in sending him over to the basement and out of harm's way.

Never.

'What you waiting for then?' said Sid as he poked the gun in Malcolm's direction. 'Get *moving*!'

'Just going, Sid.'

Malcolm turned, looked up and down the street, and crossed diagonally towards No. 33.

'Get a fucking move on or you're cat's meat!' said Sid under his breath.

The pistol was pointed directly at Malcolm's back and Sid in a way was hoping he'd pull a stroke, then he could snuff him without any compunction.

Sid consoled himself with the thought that he'd shown him who was boss in no fucking uncertain terms. You got to show these guys from time to time who rules the roost. Only language they understand.

He now thought it prudent to cover the pistol. He reached back and grabbed the Isle of Thanet map and held that over the weapon. He was safe now. Unassailable.

Malcolm had stopped at the top of the steps to the base-ment and was looking around. Down you fucking go! Go on! Down! Down there or I'm going to aerate your head!

Malcolm took a couple of steps forward, descended and disappeared from sight.

Sid smiled to himself. He was well pleased with this show of force. Well pleased.

Now I just wait.

Sit it out until he gets back and gives me the strength of it. Sit here minding my own business and waiting. Nice day. Nothing else to do.

Sid started humming again.

He reached into his pocket and took out a few tubs of pills. He didn't know what they were but he thought he'd take a few of each just to be on the safe side. He washed them down with an already opened can of Coke Malcolm had parked in a plastic can-holder that was suctioned on to the dashboard.

Sid continued humming, smiling and glancing up and down the street.

Certainly showed that asshole Malcolm who was boss, eh? Certainly showed him!

Yeah. Sure did.

Then Sid stopped humming and the colour leached from his face.

He started trembling and sweating.

The semi-psycho macho bullshit with Malcolm, sending him off like that, had blinded him to something that was now glaringly obvious.

Sid was alone.

Alone.

Sitting here alone and vulnerable and just a little unpro-tected. True, he had the 9mm, but....

Alone.

How could he have been so dumb? So stupid? How could he have blinded himself to this?

Why was it so important to send Malcolm over there *now*, this very minute? Why the manic rush? He wouldn't have behaved like that in the old days. He'd have been cautious, circumspect, patient. He'd have got some more muscle down. Planned a military-style operation. Done it right.

But he'd done it wrong.

And he was *alone*.

The trembling increased. He was shaking. Shaking like his old grandmother who had Parkinson's Disease. Visibly oscillating.

And sweating.

As wet as if he'd just stepped out of a shower.

He was paralysed with fear.

Total panic.

He screamed.

He had to do something. Get out of the van. Get out of here. Away.

Les.

Yes, Les. He's in the Merc.

Les. Salvation.

Sid was gibbering to himself as he opened the van door and swung his legs around and down.

There was the Merc up there. Its engine quietly ticking over.

Sid walked quickly and the walk soon metamorphosed into an accelerated amble. Sid wasn't in good shape. He couldn't run, but he was moving as fast as he could.

Up ahead the Merc. Yes. Away from here. I'll be all right. Got to get to the Merc.

The pistol slid away from Sid's right hand and hit the road. Sid was as unaware of this as he was of the two denim-clad, blond-haired men who were now following him. They looked like twins. They were Larry and Dirk. They were both the same height, six foot two, and both heavily suntanned. They looked like they had stepped from the posters on the wall of Tipper's basement. Two tough faggots.

Sid reached the car. He grasped the handle of the rear nearside door and opened it. There was Les and Les could deliver him from all of this. Take him away to somewhere safe and quiet. Les could do all that.

Sid fell on to the back seat and in between gasping for air managed to order Les to 'Drive! Now!'

Les turned, but it wasn't Les. It was a face that Sid had never seen before. A face that leered at him.

And then the two guys in denim got in either side of Sid. They were smiling. One of them said, 'Mr Sid, you saved us the trouble of getting you from the van.' Sid didn't hear what he said, much less notice that it was said with a Dutch accent.

Then Sid was pushed to the floor. A blindfold was put around his eyes and gaffer tape over his mouth. His arms were secured behind his back with a plastic cable-tie that drew blood. Another cable-tie was put around his ankles and this too drew blood.

Then there was laughter from the two blond guys and the Merc pulled out and headed towards the Ramsgate Road as Sid passed out.

Sid's consciousness slowly ebbed back. First he heard sounds, far-off sounds that he could not identify, then he saw light. Sunlight.

He was in an elegant nineteenth-century room. The blinds were pulled down but shafts of sunlight still managed to penetrate the cracks, gaps and edges. The furniture was all antique, the walls were covered with green silk. Oil paintings, portraits mainly, hung here and there and the room had a subtle scent of sandalwood. But, of course, Sid noticed none of this. Other things were on his mind. More pressing priorities. Though he did realise he was tightly strapped to a massive oaken chair.

Then, standing there in front of him, were Larry and Dirk. Their arms were folded and they were smiling.

A figure appeared between them. It was a man wearing

an expensive suit, a dark shirt and a bright floral tie. A red rose was in his buttonhole. Wrap-around sunglasses covered his eyes. And he wore black leather gloves. He was resting against a polished wood cane that was decorated with silver tracery.

The man took several steps forward towards Sid. Halting, unsteady steps. Steps he couldn't have made without the cane.

Sid tried to say something but the words were stillborn in his throat.

The man looked down at Sid and said in a cultured English voice that was both casual and menacing at the same time, 'I'm afraid the game's over now, Sid. We've reached the final act. You're not long for *this* world.'

Sid managed to say, 'Who are you? What's this all about?'

The man raised his right hand and removed the sunglasses. There was nothing to be seen of his right eye – just a hollow socket lined with stretched skin that had an unnatural blue tinge to it. The eye had been shot away by a bullet that had also removed part of the bone above the eye and most of the eyebrow. The scar tissue here registered the path of the projectile.

Sid shuddered

'Not only this,' said the man pointing to his face, 'but these too.' He indicated his legs. 'Very nearly useless.'

Sid looked down at the man's legs and then back at his face.

'How'd this happen then?' said Sid, perplexed as to why the figure should draw *his* attention to these infirmities.

'Very easily, Sid. It was all down to you.'

'Who are *you*?'

'I'm Simon Gould.'

'Simon Gould!? No you're not. He's dead. The fish had him.'

'The fish *nearly* had me, but as you can see I managed to survive. Though I do sometimes think I might have been better off had it all ended there.'

'Simon Gould was shot and put in a bag and then dumped. You *can't* be him.'

'But I am,' said Gould. 'I'd cut open the bag before it had hit the water. I survived. The life force is never more tenacious and determined than when it is under threat. I swam ashore...and here, well, here I am.' He laughed. A hollow laugh that confused Sid and echoed inside his head for a small eternity.

Sid was searching for some way to extricate himself from this. 'Can't we talk a deal or something? I can cut you in on what I've got going. There's plenty for both of us. You don't want to do anything to me. Do you? Eh? Do you? You...*can't*.'

'I can and I will, Sid. It is the concluding scene of the drama that began all those years ago in the Essex caravan.'

'You...you...*you* were behind all this!' shouted Sid. 'You shot Lionel and the others. It was *you*!'

'Correct, Sid. Completely correct.'

There was a silence. Then Gould continued. 'Revenge, as they say, is a dish best eaten cold. I bided my time and when the opportunity came I put a plan into action. I was patient. I was not going to be rushed into anything precipitous. I wanted you on the rack and then it was going to turn...*slowly*.'

Sid struggled with the words in his throat. 'How much money do you want? I've got plenty. You have it. I'll go away. What do you say to that, eh? We can both come out of this ahead. Right?'

Gould shook his head. 'I have a very successful business in Amsterdam. Money is not what I'm after. I've been over here since the beginning of the year supervising the building of a new yacht, right here in Ramsgate. Revenge is the only currency you and I can deal in.'

And with that Gould turned and took slow and deliberate steps across the room and through the double doors which silently closed behind him

Larry and Dirk walked towards Sid, grinning with their

dazzlingly white teeth. Just grinning and silent.

'Time to go, *yuh*?' said Larry.

Sid let out a piercing glissando scream and at the same time he pissed himself and evacuated his bowels.

He was untied from the chair and then had cable-ties put around his ankles and wrists again. He was put in a large hessian sack that was firmly tied around his neck. His mouth was stuffed with a spherical rubber object attached to straps that were secured at the back of his head. Sid would not be saying another word – ever.

Then he was blindfolded.

That night, at 10.30 p.m., just outside Ramsgate harbour the blindfold was removed. The deck of the motor launch was one of the last things Sid saw. Larry and Dirk tied weights to him as Gould watched.

Five minutes later Sid was over the side and descending through the night waters.

Even then he could not believe this was happening.

At two fathoms he was dead, but not from drowning. A massive heart attack terminated his life even before his lungs were full of water.

Thus did Sid Blattner translate out of this life.

Vince awoke on a mattress on the floor. It was cold and he pulled the duvet up over him.

He looked at the single naked light bulb that was suspended from the ceiling and then down and across at the blue bucket that was now full with his urine and excreta.

If that wasn't enough of a problem the fact that there was no longer any toilet paper left was going to ensure that today wasn't going to be easy to get through.

Not that Vince knew any more what 'day' meant.

They had taken his watch from him, along with everything else except his clothes, when they had dumped him here.

He had no way of keeping track of time. Day? Night? These were abstractions in this cold cellar. Hours?

Minutes? They meant nothing. There just seemed to be an eternal *now*.

He could have been here a day, a week, or, less likely, a month. He didn't know.

It was a never-ending present.

And they? Who were *they*?

He was knocked out, coshed over the head. He didn't remember anything about it but there was the silent testimony of the lump on his head, the ache there, and the matted blood. He remembered being in Tipper's flat, he thinks he remembers going to leave it and then – nothing. Nothing until waking up here.

He never saw anyone. There or here.

So he doesn't know who *they* are.

But he does know they exist.

Because, every so often, if he goes around the corner and ascends the naked stone steps to the vast oaken door at the top there is some food and something to drink. *Somebody* must put it through the cat flap.

Someone.

They.

Mind you the food isn't fancy. Apples, oranges, corned beef, bread, biscuits and, on one occasion, a Big Mac, French fries and a chocolate shake.

Not fancy, but enough to keep you going.

The drink was usually a bottle of mineral water, though he had had some cans of soft drink.

It definitely wasn't a woman who was doing the catering around here.

Vince turned over and tried to get back to sleep. He couldn't. He was tired and needed the sleep but he was awake. Wide awake.

And he was hungry.

He pushed back the duvet and reached for his trousers, socks and shoes. He put them on and shuffled across the bare floor to the steps.

What's on the menu today? he thought as he wearily

climbed the steps. Digestive biscuits and a cup of cold water?

Vince stopped.

There was a plate in front of the cat flap and on it was a can of lager against which was propped an envelope with the word *Vince* written in black ink. He reached forward and picked up the envelope. It was one of those almost square envelopes made of expensive paper you see in the Stationery Department at Harrods.

Vince opened the envelope and took out a single sheet of matching notepaper, about two-thirds A4 in size. The writing was the same as on the envelope, a handsome italic hand. The note read:

Monday

Vince:

*Sid is dead and the tale played
out. You are free to go.
Your survival is proof to myself
that my revenge was not blind
(besides, you weren't on the
shooting party, were you?).
God be with you.*

There was no signature or name on the letter, instead there was a simple line drawing of a scorpion at the foot of the page. Vince checked the envelope again. Nothing there either.

Then Vince noticed the door was open a few inches. Was he free to go or was this part of some ruse?

He pushed the door open a few more inches. Further steps led up to a partially opened door through which light was showing.

Vince went back down the steps and collected his jacket which he had been using as a pillow. He climbed the steps in twos and pushed the oaken door open. He walked through and up the further set of steps. The door at the top opened on to the hallway of a large house. There was fine period furniture and expensive carpeting. Several oil paintings were on the walls. Bright sunlight was streaming through the stained glass either side and above the front door of the house.

There was the sound of seagulls.

Then Vince heard the sound of a human voice. He turned and saw a suited figure walking down the corridor towards him holding a clipboard in one hand and a mobile telephone to his ear in the other. The figure had an air of middle-class condescension about him (not to mention quiffed, bouffant hair) and he looked a dead-ringer for that smooth Tory geezer, Michael Portillo, *and* sounded like him too as he spoke loudly into the phone: 'Inventory all appears to be in order. Little wear and tear to the shower cubicle, but otherwise, tickety-boo. I'll be expecting them here tomorrow at about noon, so if you can pass that on to Archie I'd be most obliged.'

Portillo then stopped dead when he saw Vince ahead of him: the dirty, unshaven epitome of the lower orders.

'I say, what on earth do *you* think you're doing *here*!'

Vince grinned and said, 'Well, actually, old chap I was just going to have a quick wank over the carpet.'

Portillo strode towards Vince. He was shouting now. 'I'm having *you* out of here this very minute!'

Vince stood his ground. Portillo arrived and prodded him in the chest with the mobile telephone. Vince grabbed his wrist, removed the mobile phone, dropped it to the ground and stamped on it. Vince now twisted his wrist round so Portillo had his back to him and then he kicked him. He fell forward and hit his face against the banister. He let out a cry and then began sobbing. 'You've broken my nose!'

Vince then grabbed Portillo, pushed him against the stairs and put his knee into his back. 'Who lives here?'

'Nobody!' cried Portillo.

Vince repeated the question and dug his knee in deeper.

'Nobody! We manage it for the Trust. We rent it out!'

'In that case, who's *been* here then?' Vince demanded.

'Gould. A Mr Simon Gould.'

Simon Gould?

The Simon Gould?

Simon the Scorpian?

Simon the Scorpian. They all called him that even before
Phil tumbled him, not just because he was born under the
sign of Scorpio (thusly a Scorp*ian*) but because they figured
he was a scorp*ion*. Vince was the last one to sus old Simon
before the news got through to Sid who, right up until the
end, wouldn't hear a word against the guy.

Him?

But didn't Sid and the lads do him in out Essex way? In
a caravan wasn't it? Christ, Vince had heard the story
enough times. Had Sid and the others got the wrong guy
or what? Had they even fucked *that* up? Botched *that*? Had
they…?

Vince was out of the country at the time, taking a long
holiday in Miami with his wife and kid. The whole Simon
the Scorpian thing had blown up soon after he had left
London. By the time he got back, two months later, it was
ancient history…or so Sid reckoned. Well, what the fuck?
Who cares now? It is history, finally. And Sid too.

Could there be two guys with the same – forget it! There's
only one Simon Gould. Only one Simon the Scorpian….

Vince had never had much to do with the Scorpian.
They were both working in different areas for Sid. He'd
always been pleasant enough when Vince had met him at
one of the clubs or wherever and, indeed, Vince had never
suspected anything untoward, not until the end when Phil
put him in the picture….

Vince took his knee out of Portillo's back and walked
across the hall to the sounds of sobbing and whimpering.
He opened the front door. It was a fine, sunny day with a

clear blue sky and there at his feet was Ramsgate Harbour, its stone walls arcing round and embracing the craft tethered to its jetties. The seagulls were circling overhead in endless spirals and crying that cry that so distinguishes the seaside.

Vince looked at the letter again, and the envelope. There were a thousand answers he didn't know, but he no longer wanted to know. Indeed, he was no longer even interested in posing the questions.

He tore the letter and the envelope up into fifty small pieces and threw them in the air.

He had his life back. What more did he want?

Next stop, Wells-next-the-Sea.

This here was already history. It really was.

He was on his way.

But first, give Marilyn a call. The girl from the Tivoli Ballroom.

Perhaps she'd like a break? Perhaps she'd like a little holiday up there?

Vince felt sure she would.

10: L'Envoi

YES, THE DRAMA IS DONE, but what of the other players on the stage? Whence we know, but whither now?

CANDY GREEN lives in Lewisham, South London, and shares a flat with Sheryll Adibe, a Nigerian. They advertise their services in local telephone booths as 'The Black and White Massage Twins', strictly for 'gentlemen who can afford the best'.

SIMON GOULD returned to Amsterdam in his new yacht. He continues to run a very profitable business exporting pornography, chiefly to England, and drugs to wherever there is a demand. Larry and Dirk are never far from his side.

MALCOLM went straight back to London after he left Ramsgate, then he went straight *period*, and has kept out of harm's way since then running a small decorating business in Sandy, Bedfordshire.

LES or, rather, what's left of him continues to 'sleep with the fishes' in Pegwell Bay to the west of Ramsgate.

HARRY THE CHAUFFEUR, who had a gun shoved into his ribs by Dirk on Marine Terrace, Margate, was taken away in a van and shot in the head. His body was dumped down a deep septic tank on a farm near the village of Minster on the other side of Thanet.

TERRY AVELING managed to ensure that none of his complicity or moonlighting activities were ever known to his superiors. He is due to take early retirement next year and would like to open a small guest house somewhere down Cornwall way.

MIRIAM BLATTNER managed to salt enough of Sid's money away to live a life free of financial worry. She divides her time between Florida and Israel and sees herself as misunderstood as her all-time *fave* heroine – Dame Shirley Porter.

LENNY TIPPER co-owns a small hotel in Bangkok that caters to English and American paedophiles on holiday. He also produces home-made porno videos that are released on his BoyLove (*sic*) label.

WALLY SLADE's new proprietor gave him the push and a handsome payoff. He moved to the Suffolk coast and produces ghosted memoirs for Scotland Yard detectives and the occasional volume of his own reminiscences, works in every instance that might better qualify for the fiction rather than non-fiction shelves.

RAY SEAGO recovered from his depressions thanks to Prozac. He now has a small farm near Woodchurch, Kent, and plays a lot of golf. He thinks all 'wogs' must be repatriated and that 'Lord' Jeffrey Archer should be running the country.

DANNY HOPE …well, you all see him popping up on television these days as an 'actor' playing roles that supposedly reflect his off screen persona. A sad case.

BRIAN SPINKS found himself out of a job after Sid's demise. He was last heard of working as a minicab controller somewhere on the Seven Sisters Road and fiddling the Social.

MRS SPOONER won a few thousand pounds on the Lottery and now works three mornings a week at the local Help the Genteel Mentally Unstable charity shop in Cliftonville.

CHIEF-SUPERINTENDENT LUCKSFORD is currently helping the police with their inquiries – specifically, an internal investigation regarding his dealings with a known money launderer. The future looks bleak, but his pension is safe.